LILLIAN MORRIS
AND OTHER STORIES

LILLIAN MORRIS AND OTHER STORIES

BY·HENRYK·SIENKIEWICZ
AVTHOR ··· OF ··· "WITH
FIRE·AND·SWORD"·ETC·
TRANSLATED ··BY
JEREMIAH·CVRTIN·WITH
ILLVSTRATIONS · BY
EDMVND·H·GARRETT

Fredonia Books
Amsterdam, The Netherlands

Lillian Morris and Other Stories

by
Henryk Sienkiewicz

ISBN: 1-4101-0074-X

Reprinted from the 1894 edition

Fredonia Books
Amsterdam, The Netherlands
http://www.fredoniabooks.com

In order to make original editions of historical works available to scholars at an economical price, this facsimile of the original edition of 1894 is reproduced from the best available copy and has been digitally enhanced to improve legibility, but the text remains unaltered to retain historical authenticity.

Contents.

The Captain

LILLIAN MORRIS OF BOSTON

LILLIAN MORRIS.

DURING my stay in California I went with my worthy and gallant friend, Captain R., to visit Y., a compatriot of ours who was living in the secluded mountains of Santa Lucia. Not finding him at home, we passed five days in a lonely ravine, in company with an old Indian servant, who during his master's absence took care of the Angora goats and the bees.

Conforming to the ways of the country, I spent the hot summer days mainly in sleep, but when night came I sat down near a fire of dry "chamisal," and listened to stories from the captain, concerning his wonderful adventures, and events which could happen only in the wilds of America.

Those hours passed for me very bewitchingly. The nights were real Californian: calm, warm, starry; the fire burned cheerily, and in its gleam I saw the gigantic, but shapely and noble form of the old pioneer warrior. Raising his eyes to the stars, he sought to recall past events, cherished names, and dear faces, the very remembrance of which brought a mild sadness to his features. Of these narratives I give one just as I heard it, thinking that the reader will listen to it with as much interest as I did.

CHAPTER I

I CAME to America in September, 1849, said
the captain, and found myself in New Orleans,
which was half French at that time. From
New Orleans I went up the Mississippi to a
great sugar plantation, where I found work and
good wages. But since I was young in those
days, and full of daring, sitting in one spot and
writing annoyed me; so I left that place soon
and began life in the forest. My comrades
and I passed some time among the lakes of
Louisiana, in the midst of crocodiles, snakes,

and mosquitoes. We supported ourselves with
hunting and fishing, and from time to time
floated down great numbers of logs to New
Orleans, where purchasers paid for them not
badly in money.

Our expeditions reached distant places. We
went as far as "Bloody Arkansas," which,
sparsely inhabited even at this day, was well-
nigh a pure wilderness then. Such a life, full
of labors and dangers, bloody encounters with
pirates on the Mississippi, and with Indians,
who at that time were numerous in Louisiana,
Arkansas, and Tennessee, increased my health
and strength, which by nature were uncommon,
and gave me also such knowledge of the plains,
that I could read in that great book not worse
than any red warrior.

After the discovery of gold in California,
large parties of emigrants left Boston, New
York, Philadelphia, and other eastern cities
almost daily, and one of these, thanks to my
reputation, chose me for leader, or as we say,
captain.

I accepted the office willingly, since wonders
were told of California in those days, and I had
cherished thoughts of going to the Far West,
though without concealing from myself the
perils of the journey.

At present the distance between New York
and San Francisco is passed by rail in a week,
and the real desert begins only west of Omaha;
in those days it was something quite different.
Cities and towns, which between New York and
Chicago are as numerous as poppy-seeds now,
did not exist then; and Chicago itself, which
later on grew up like a mushroom after rain, was
merely a poor obscure fishing-village not found
on maps. It was necessary to travel with wagons,
men, and mules through a country quite wild,
and inhabited by terrible tribes of Indians:
Crows, Blackfeet, Pawnees, Sioux, and Aricka-
rees, which it was well-nigh impossible to avoid
in large numbers, since those tribes, movable
as sand, had no fixed dwellings, but, being hun-
ters, circled over great spaces of prairie, while
following buffaloes and antelopes.

Not few were the toils, then, that threatened us; but he who goes to the Far West must be ready to suffer hardship, and expose his life frequently. I feared most of all the responsibility which I had accepted. This matter had been settled, however, and there was nothing to do but make preparations for the road. These lasted more than two months, since we had to bring wagons, even from Pittsburgh, to buy mules, horses, arms, and collect large supplies of provisions. Toward the end of winter, however, all things were ready.

I wished to start in such season as to pass the great prairies lying between the Mississippi and the Rocky Mountains in spring, for I knew that in summer because of heat in those open places, multitudes of men died of various diseases. I decided for this reason to lead the train, not over the southern route by St. Louis, but through Iowa, Nebraska, and Northern Colorado. That road was more dangerous with reference to Indians, but beyond doubt it was the healthier. The plan roused opposition at first among people of the train. I declared that if they would not obey they might choose another captain. They yielded after a brief consultation, and we moved at the first breath of spring.

Days now set in which for me were toilsome enough, especially till such time as men had grown accustomed to me and the conditions of the journey. It is true that my person roused confidence, for my daring trips to Arkansas had won a certain fame among the restless population of the border, and the name of "Big Ralph," by which I was known on the prairies, had struck the ears of most of my people more than once. In general, however, the captain, or leader, was, from the nature of things, in a very critical position frequently with regard to emigrants. It was my duty to choose the camping-ground every evening, watch over the advance in the daytime, have an eye on the whole caravan, which extended at times a mile over the prairie, appoint sentries at the halting-places, and give men permission to rest in the wagons when their turn came.

Americans have in them, it is true, the spirit of organization developed to a high degree ; but in toils on the road men's energies weaken, and unwillingness seizes the most enduring. At such times no one wishes to reconnoitre on horseback all day and stand sentry at night, but each man would like to evade the turn which is coming to him, and lie whole days in a wagon. Besides, in intercourse with Yankees, a captain must know how to reconcile discipline with a certain social familiarity, — a thing far from easy. In time of march, and in the hours of night-watching, I was perfect master of the will of each of my companions ; but during rest in the day at farms and settlements, to which we came at first on the road, my rôle of commander ended. Each man was master of himself then, and more than once I was forced to overcome the opposition of insolent adventurers; but when in presence of numerous spectators it turned out a number of times that my Mazovian fist was the stronger, my significance rose, and later on I never had personal encounters. Besides, I knew American character thoroughly. I knew how to help myself, and, in addition to all, my endurance and willingness were increased by a certain pair of blue eyes, which looked out at me with special interest from beneath the canvas roof of a wagon. Those eyes looked from under a forehead shaded by rich golden hair, and they belonged to a maiden named Lillian Morris. She was delicate, slender, with finely cut features, and a face thoughtful, though almost childlike. That seriousness in such a young girl struck me at once when beginning the journey, but duties connected with the office of captain soon turned my mind and attention elsewhere.

During the first weeks I exchanged with Miss Morris barely a couple of words beyond

the usual daily " good morning." Taking compassion, however, on her youth and loneliness, —
she had no relatives in that caravan, — I showed
the poor girl some trifling services. I had not
the least need of guarding her with my authority
of leader nor with my fist from the forwardness
of young men in the train, for among Americans even the youngest woman is sure, if not
of the over-prompt politeness for which the
French are distinguished, at least of perfect
security. In view, however, of Lillian's delicate
health, I put her in the most commodious
wagon, in charge of a driver of great experience, named Smith. I spread for her a couch
on which she could sleep with comfort ; finally,
I lent her a warm buffalo-skin, of which I
had a number in reserve. Though these services were not important, Lillian seemed to
feel a lively gratitude, and omitted no opportunity to show it. She was evidently a very
mild and retiring person. Two women, Aunt
Grosvenor and Aunt Atkins, soon loved her

beyond expression for the sweetness of her character. "Little Bird," a title which they gave her, became the name by which she was known in the caravan. Still, there was not the slightest approach between Little Bird and me, till I noticed that the blue and almost angelic eyes of that maiden were turned toward me, with a peculiar sympathy and determined interest.

That might have been interpreted in this way: Among all the people of the train I alone had some social refinement; Lillian, in whom also a careful training was evident, saw in me, therefore, a man nearer to her than the rest of the company. But I understood the affair somewhat differently. The interest which she showed pleased my vanity; my vanity made me pay her more attention, and look oftener into her eyes. It was not long till I was striving in vain to discover why, up to that time, I had paid so little attention to a person so exquisite, — a person who might inspire tender feelings in any man who had a heart.

Thenceforth I was fond of coursing around her wagon on my horse. During the heat of the day, which in spite of the early spring annoyed us greatly at noon, the mules dragged forward lazily, and the caravan stretched along the prairie, so that a man standing at the first wagon could barely see the last one. Often did I fly at such times from end to end, wearying my horse without need, just to see that bright head in passing, and those eyes, which hardly ever left my mind. At first my imagination was more taken than my heart; I received pleasant solace from the thought that among those strange people I was not entirely a stranger, since a sympathetic little soul was occupied with me somewhat. Perhaps this came not from vanity, but from the yearning which on earth a man feels to discover his own self in a heart near to him, to fix his affections and thoughts on one living beloved existence, instead of wasting them on such indefinite, general objects as plains and forests, and losing himself in remotenesses and infinities.

I felt less lonely then, and the whole journey took on attractions unknown to me hitherto. Formerly, when the caravan stretched out on the prairie, as I have described, so that the last wagons vanished from the eye, I saw in that only a lack of attention, and disorder, from which I grew very angry. Now, when I halted on some eminence, the sight of those wagons white and striped, shone on by the sun and plunging in the sea of grass, like ships on the ocean, the sight of men, on horseback and armed, scattered in picturesque disorder at the sides of the wagons, filled my soul with delight and happiness. And I know not whence such comparisons came to me, but that seemed some kind of Old Testament procession, which I, like a patriarch, was leading to the Promised Land. The bells on the harness of the mules and the drawling, " Get up ! " of the drivers accompanied like music thoughts which came from my heart and my nature.

But I did not pass from that dialogue of eyes with Lillian to another, for the presence of the women travelling with her prevented me. Still, from the time when I saw that there was something between us for which I could not find a name yet, though I felt that the something was there, a certain strange timidity seized me. I redoubled, however, my care for the women, and frequently I looked into the wagon, inquiring about the health of Aunt Atkins and Aunt Grosvenor, so as to justify in that way and equalize the attentions with which I surrounded Lillian ; but she understood my methods perfectly, and this understanding became as it were our own secret, concealed from the rest of the people.

Soon, glances and a passing exchange of words and tender endeavors were not enough for me. That young maiden with bright hair and sweet look drew me to her with an irresistible power. I began to think of her whole days; and at night, when wearied from visiting the sentries, and hoarse from crying "All is well!" I came at last to the wagon, and wrapping myself in a buffalo-skin, closed my eyes to rest, it seemed to me that the gnats and mosquitoes buzzing around were singing unceasingly in my ears, "Lillian! Lillian! Lillian!" Her form stood before me in my dreams; at waking, my first thought flew to her like a swallow; and still, wonderful thing! I had not noticed that the dear attraction which everything assumed for me, that painting in the soul of objects in golden colors, and those thoughts sailing after her wagon, were not a friendship nor an inclination for an orphan, but a mightier feeling by far, a feeling from which no man on earth can defend himself when the turn has come to him.

It may be that I should have noticed this sooner, had it not been that the sweetness of Lillian's nature won every one to her; I thought, therefore, that I was no more under the charm of that maiden than were others. All loved her as their own child, and I had proof of this before my eyes daily. Her companions were simple women, sufficiently inclined to wordy quarrels, and still, more than once had I seen Aunt Atkins, the greatest Herod on earth, combing Lillian's hair in the morning, kissing her with the affection of a mother; sometimes I saw Aunt Grosvenor warming in her own palms the maiden's hands, which had chilled in the night. The men surrounded her likewise with care and attentions. There was a certain Henry Simpson in the train, a young adventurer from Kansas, a fearless hunter and an honest fellow at heart, but so self-sufficient, so insolent and rough, that during the first month I had to beat the man twice, to convince him that there was some one in the train with a stronger hand than his, and of superior significance. You should have seen that same Henry Simpson speaking to Lillian. He who would not have thought anything of the President of the United States himself, lost in her presence all his confidence and boldness, and repeated every moment, " I beg your pardon, Miss Morris ! " He had quite the bearing of a chained mastiff, but clearly the mastiff was ready to obey every motion of that small, half-childlike hand. At the halting-places he tried always to be with Lillian, so as to render her various little services. He lighted the fire, and selected for her a place free from smoke, covering it first with moss and then with his own horse-blankets; he chose for her the best pieces of game, doing all this with a certain timid attention which I had not thought to find in him, and which roused in me, nevertheless, a kind of ill-will very similar to jealousy.

But I could only be angry, nothing more. Henry, if the turn to stand guard did not come to him, might do what he liked with

his time, hence he could be near Lillian,
while my turn of service never ended. On
the road the wagons dragged forward one
after another, often very far apart ; but when
we entered an open country for the midday
rest I placed the wagons, according to prairie
custom, in a line side by side, so that a man
could hardly push between them. It is
difficult to understand how much trouble and
toil I had before such an easily defended
line was formed. Mules are by nature wild
and untractable ; either they balked, or would
not go out of the beaten track, biting each
other meanwhile, neighing and kicking ;
wagons, twisted by sudden movement, were
turned over frequently, and the raising up
of such real houses of wood and canvas took
no little time ; the braying of mules, the
cursing of drivers, the tinkling of bells, the
barking of dogs which followed us, caused
a hellish uproar. When I had brought all
into order in some fashion. I had to oversee

the unharnessing of the animals and urge on the men whose work it was to drive them to pasture and then to water. Meanwhile men who during the advance had gone out on the prairie to hunt, were returning from all sides with game; the fires were occupied by people, and I found barely time to eat and draw breath.

I had almost double labor when we started after each rest, for attaching the mules involved more noise and uproar than letting them out. Besides, the drivers tried always to get ahead of one another, so as to spare themselves trouble in turning out of line in bad places. From this came quarrels and disputes, together with curses and unpleasant delays on the road. I had to watch over all this, and in time of marching ride in advance, immediately after the guides, to examine the neighborhood and select in season defensible places, abounding in water, and, in general, commodious for night camps.

Frequently I cursed my duties as captain, though on the other hand the thought filled me with pride, that in all that boundless desert I was the first before the desert itself, before people, before Lillian, and that the fate of all those beings, wandering behind the wagons over that prairie, was placed in my hands.

CHAPTER II

ON a certain time, after we had passed the Mississippi, we halted for the night at Cedar River, the banks of which, grown over with cottonwood, gave us assurance of fuel for the night. While returning from the men on duty, who had gone into the thicket with axes, I saw, from a distance, that our people, taking advantage of the beautiful weather and the calm fair day, had wandered out on the prairie in every direction. It was very early; we halted for the night usually about five o'clock in the afternoon, so as to move in the morning at daybreak.   Soon I met Miss Morris.   I dismounted immediately, and leading my horse by the bridle, approached the young lady, happy that I could be alone with her even for a while.   I inquired then why she, so young and unattended, had undertaken a journey which might wear out the strongest man.

"Never should I have consented to receive you into our caravan," said I, "had I not thought during the first few days of our journey that you were the daughter of Aunt Atkins; now it is too late to turn back.   But will you be strong enough, my dear child? You must be ready to find the journey hereafter less easy than hitherto."

"I know all this," answered she, without raising her pensive blue eyes, "but I must go on, and I am happy indeed that I cannot go back.   My father is in California, and from the letter which he sent me by way of Cape Horn. I learn that for some months he has

been ill of a fever in Sacramento. Poor father !
he was accustomed to comfort and my care, —
and it was only through love of me that he
went to California. I do not know whether I
shall find him alive ; but I feel that in going
to him, I am only fulfilling a duty that is
dear to me."

There was no answer to such words ; moreover, all that I might object to this undertak-
ing would be too late. I inquired then of
Lillian for nearer details touching her father.
These she gave with great pleasure, and I
learned that in Boston Mr. Morris had been
judge of the Supreme Court, or highest tribunal
of the State ; that he had lost his property,
and had gone to the newly discovered mines
of California in the hope of acquiring a new
fortune, and bringing back to his daughter,
whom he loved more than life, her former
social position. Meanwhile, he caught a
fever in the unwholesome Sacramento valley,
and judging that he should die he sent Lillian

his last blessing. She sold all the property
that he had left with her, and resolved to
hasten to him. At first she intended to go
by sea; but an acquaintance with Aunt Atkins
made by chance two days before the caravan
started, changed her mind.   Aunt Atkins,
who was from Tennessee, having had her ears
filled with tales which friends of mine from
the banks of the Mississippi had told her
and others of my daring expeditions to the
famed Arkansas, of my experience in jour-
neys over the prairies, and the care which I
gave to the weak (this I consider as a simple
duty), described me in such colors before
Lillian that the girl, without hesitating longer,
joined the caravan going under my leadership.
To those exaggerated narratives of Aunt
Atkins, who did not delay to add that I was
of noble birth, it is necessary to ascribe the
fact that Miss Morris was occupied with my
person.

"You may be sure," said I, when she had

finished her story, "that no one will do you any wrong here, and that care will not fail you; as to your father, California is the healthiest country on earth, and no one dies of fever there. In every case, while I am alive, you will not be left alone; and meanwhile may God bless your sweet face!"

"Thank you, captain," answered she, with emotion, and we went on; but my heart beat with more violence. Gradually our conversation became livelier, and no one could foresee that that sky above us would become cloudy.

"But all here are kind to you, Miss Morris?" asked I again, not supposing that just that question would be the cause of misunderstanding.

"Oh yes, all," said she, "and Aunt Atkins and Aunt Grosvenor, and Henry Simpson too is very good."

This mention of Simpson pained me suddenly, like the bite of a snake.

"Henry is a mule-driver," answered I curtly, "and has to care for the wagons."

But Lillian, occupied with the course of her own thoughts, had not noticed the change in my voice, and spoke on as if to herself, —

"He has an honest heart, and I shall be grateful to him all my life."

"Miss Morris," interrupted I, cut to the quick, "you may even give him your hand. I wonder, however, that you choose me as a confidant of your feelings."

When I said that she looked at me with astonishment but made no reply, and we went on together in disagreeable silence. I knew not what to say, though my heart was full of bitterness and anger toward her and myself. I felt simply conquered by jealousy of Simpson, but still I could not fight against it. The position seemed to me so unendurable that I said all at once briefly and dryly, —

"Good night, Miss Morris!"

"Good night," answered she calmly, turning her head to hide two tears that were dropping down her cheeks.

I mounted my horse and rode away again toward the point whence the sound of axes came, and where, among others, Henry Simpson was cutting a cottonwood. After a while I was seized by a certain measureless regret, for it seemed to me that those two tears were falling on my heart. I turned my horse, and next minute I was near Lillian a second time.

"Why are you crying, Miss Morris?" asked I.

"Oh, sir," said she, "I know that you are of a noble family, Aunt Atkins told me that, and you have been so kind to me."

She did everything not to cry; but she could not restrain herself, and could not finish her answer, for tears choked her voice. The poor thing! she had been touched to the bottom of her pensive soul by my answer regarding Simpson, for there was evident in it a certain aristocratic contempt; but I was not even dreaming of aristocracy, — I

was simply jealous; and now, seeing her so
unhappy, I wanted to seize my own collar
and throttle myself. Grasping her hand, I
said with animation : —

"Lillian, Lillian, you did not understand me.
I take God to witness that no pride was speaking through me. Look at me : I have nothing
in the world but these two hands, — what is my
descent to me? Something else pained me,
and I wanted to go away; but I could not
support your tears. And I swear to you also,
that what I have said to you pains me more
than it does you. You are not an object of
indifference to me, Lillian. Oh, not at all !
for if you were, what you think of Henry
would not concern me. He is an honest
fellow, but that does not touch the question.
You see how much your tears cost me ;
then forgive me as sincerely as I entreat your
forgiveness."

Speaking in this way I raised her hand and
pressed it to my lips; that high proof of re-

spect, and the truthfulness which sounded in
my request, succeeded in quieting the maiden
somewhat. She did not cease at once to
weep, but her tears were of another kind,
for a smile was visible through them, as a
sun-ray through mist. Something too was
sticking in my throat, and I could not stifle
my emotion. A certain tender feeling mastered my heart. We walked on in silence,
and round about us the world was pleasant
and sweet.

Meanwhile, the day was inclining toward
evening; the weather was beautiful, and in
the air, already dusky, there was so much
light that the whole prairie, the distant groups
of cottonwood-trees, the wagons in our train,
and the flocks of wild geese flying northward through the sky, seemed golden and
rosy. Not the least wind moved the grass;
from a distance came to us the sound of
rapids, which the Cedar River formed in that
place, and the neighing of horses from the

direction of the camp. That evening with
such charms, that virgin land, and the presence of Lillian, brought me to such a state
of mind that my soul was almost ready to fly
out of me somewhere to the sky. I thought
myself a shaken bell, as it were. At moments
I wanted to take Lillian's hand again, raise it
to my lips, and not put it down for a long
time; but I feared lest this might offend her.
Meanwhile she walked on near me, calm, mild,
and thoughtful. Her tears had dried already;
at moments she raised her bright eyes to
me; then we began to speak again, — and
so reached the camp.

That day, in which I had experienced so
many emotions, was to end joyfully, for the
people, pleased with the beautiful weather,
had resolved to have a "picnic," or open air
festival. After a supper more abundant than
usual, one great fire was kindled, before which
there was to be dancing. Henry Simpson had
cleared away the grass purposely from a space

of many square yards, and sprinkled it with
sand brought from Cedar River. When the
spectators had assembled on the place thus
prepared, Simpson began to dance a jig, with
the accompaniment of negro flutes, to the
admiration of all. With hands hanging at
his sides he kept his whole body motionless;
but his feet were working so nimbly, striking
the ground in turn with heel and toe, that
their movement could hardly be followed by
the eye.

Meanwhile the flutes played madly; a second dancer came out, a third, then a fourth, —
and the fun was universal. The audience joined the negroes who were playing on the flutes,
and thrummed on tin pans, intended for wash-
ing the gold-bearing earth, or kept time with
pieces of ox-ribs held between the fingers of
each hand, which gave out a sound like the
clatter of castanets.

Suddenly the cry of "minstrels! minstrels!"
was heard through the whole camp. The audi-

ence formed a circle around the dancing-place;
into this stepped our negroes, Jim and Crow.
Jim held a little drum covered with snake-
skin, Crow the pieces of ox-rib mentioned
already.   For a time they stared at each other,
rolling the whites of their eyes; then they
began to sing a negro song, interrupted by
stamping and violent springs of the body; at
times the song was sad, at times wild.   The
prolonged "Dinah! ah! ah!" with which
each verse ended, changed at length into a
shout, and almost into a howling like that of
beasts.   As the dancers warmed up and grew
excited, their movements became wilder, and
at last they fell to butting each other with
blows from which European skulls would have
cracked like nutshells.   Those black figures,
shone upon by the bright gleam of the fire
and springing in wild leaps, presented a spectacle truly fantastic.   With their shouts and
the sounds of the drum, pipes, and tin pans,
and the click of the bones, were mingled

shouts of the spectators : " Hurrah for Jim !
Hurrah for Crow ! " and then shots from
revolvers.

When at last the black men were wearied
and had fallen on the ground, they began to
labor with their breasts and to pant. I commanded to give each a drink of brandy; this
put them on their feet again. But at that
moment the people began to call for a
"speech." In an instant the uproar and
music ceased. I had to drop Lillian's arm,
climb to the seat of a wagon, and turn to
those present. When I looked from my
height on those forms illuminated by the
fires, forms large, broad-shouldered, bearded,
with knives at their girdles, and hats with torn
crowns, it seemed to me that I was in some
theatre, or had become a chieftain of robbers.
They were honest brave hearts, however, though
the rough life of more than one of these men
was stormy perhaps and half wild; but here
we formed, as it were, a little world torn away

from the rest of society and confined to ourselves, destined to a common fate and threatened by common dangers. Here shoulder had to touch shoulder; each felt that he was brother to the next man; the roadless places and boundless deserts with which we were surrounded commanded those hardy miners to love one another. The sight of Lillian, the poor defenceless maiden, fearless among them and safe as if under her father's roof, brought those thoughts to my head; hence I told everything, just as I felt it, and as befitted a soldier leader who was at the same time a brother of wanderers. Every little while they interrupted me with cries: "Hurrah for the Pole! Hurrah for the captain! Hurrah for Big Ralph!" and with clapping of hands; but what made me happiest of all was to see between the network of those sunburnt strong hands one pair of small palms, rosy with the gleam of the fire and flying like a pair of white doves.

I felt then at once, What care I for the
desert, the wild beasts, the Indians and the
" outlaws "? and cried with mighty ardor,
" I will conquer anything, I will kill anything
that comes in my way, and lead the train even
to the end of the earth, — and may God
forget my right hand, if this is not true ! "
A still louder " Hurrah ! " answered these
words, and all began to sing with great enthusiasm the emigrants' song : " I crossed
the Mississippi, I will cross the Missouri."
Then Smith, the oldest among the emigrants,
a miner from near Pittsburgh in Pennsylvania,
spoke in answer.   He thanked me in the
name of the whole company, and lauded my
skill in leading the caravan. After Smith,
from nearly every wagon a man spoke. Some
made very amusing remarks, for instance
Henry Simpson, who cried out every little
while :   " Gentlemen !   I 'll be hanged if I
don't tell the truth ! " When the speakers
had grown hoarse at last, the flutes sounded,

the bones rattled, and the men began to
dance a jig again.

Night had fallen completely; the moon came
out in the sky and shone so brightly that the
flame of the fires almost paled before its
gleams; the people and the wagons were
illuminated doubly by a red and a white
light. That was a beautiful night. The
uproar of our camp offered a strange but
pleasing contrast to the calmness and deep
slumber of the prairie.

Taking Lillian's arm, I went with her
around the whole camp; our gaze passed
from the fires to the distance, and was lost
in the waves of the tall and dark grasses of
the prairie, silvery from the rays of the moon
and as mysterious as spirits. We strolled
alone in that way. Meanwhile, at one of the
fires, two Scottish Highlanders began to play
on pipes their plaintive air of " Bonnie
Dundee." We both stopped at a distance and
listened for some time in silence : all at once

I looked at Lillian, she dropped her eyes, —
and without knowing myself why I did so, I
pressed to my heart long and powerfully that
hand which she had rested on my arm. In
Lillian too the poor heart began to beat with
such force that I felt it as clearly as if on
my palm; we trembled, for we saw that
something was rising between us, that that
something was conquering, and that we would
not be to each other as we had been hitherto.
As to me I was swimming already whitherso-
ever that current was bearing me. I forgot that
the night was so bright, that the fires were not
distant, and that there were people around
them; and I wanted to fall at her feet at once,
or at least to look into her eyes. But she,
though leaning on my arm, turned her head,
as if glad to hide her face in the shade. I
wished to speak but could not; for it seemed
to me that I should call out with some voice
not my own, or if I should say the words
"I love" to Lillian I should drop to the

earth. I was not bold, being young then, and was led not by my thoughts simply, but by my soul too; and I felt this also clearly, that if I should say " I love," a curtain would fall on my past; one door would close and another would open, through which I should pass into a certain new region. Hence, though I saw happiness beyond that threshold I halted, for this very reason it may be, — that the brightness beating from out that place dazzled me. Besides, when loving comes not from the lips, but the heart, there is perhaps nothing so difficult to speak about.

I had dared to press Lillian's hand to my breast; we were silent, for I had not the boldness to mention love, and I had no wish to speak of aught else, — it was impossible at such a time.

It ended with this, that we both raised our heads and looked at the stars, like people who are praying. Then some one at the great fire called me; we returned; the festival had closed, but to end it worthily and well, the emigrants had determined to sing a psalm before going to rest. The men had uncovered their heads, and though among them were persons of various faiths, all knelt on the grass of the prairie and began to sing the psalm, "Wandering in the Wilderness." The sight was impressive. At moments of rest the silence became so perfect that the crackling of sparks in the fire could be heard, and from the river the sound of the waterfalls came to us.

Kneeling near Lillian, I looked once or twice at her face; her eyes were uplifted and wonderfully shining, her hair was a little disarranged; and, singing the hymn with devotion, she was so like an angel, that it seemed almost possible to pray to her.

After the psalm, the people went to their wagons. I, according to custom, repaired to the sentries, and then to my rest, like the others. But this time when the mosquitoes began to sing

in my ears, as they did every evening, " Lillian !
Lillian ! Lillian ! " I knew that in that wagon
beyond there was sleeping the sight of my eye
and the soul of my soul, and that in all the
world there was nothing dearer to me than
that maiden.

CHAPTER III

AT dawn the following day we passed Cedar River successfully and came out on a level, broad prairie, stretching between that river and the Winnebago, which curved imperceptibly to the south, toward the belt of forests lying along the lower boundary of Iowa. From the morning Lillian had not dared to look in my eyes. I saw that she was thoughtful; it seemed as though she were ashamed of some-thing, or troubled for some cause; but still what sin had we committed the evening be-

fore? She scarcely left the wagon. Aunt
Atkins and Aunt Grosvenor, thinking that she
was ill, surrounded her with care and tenderness. I alone knew what that meant, — that it
was neither weakness, nor pangs of conscience;
it was the struggle of an innocent being with
the presentiment that a power new and unknown
is bearing it, like a leaf, to some place far
away. It was a clear insight that there was
no help, and that sooner or later she would
have to weaken and yield to the will of that
power, forget everything, — and only love.

A pure soul draws back and is afraid on the
threshold of love, but feeling that it will cross, it
weakens. Lillian therefore was as if wearied
by a dream; but when I understood all that,
the breath in my breast was nearly stopped from
joy. I know not whether it was an honorable
feeling, but when in the morning I flew past her
wagon and saw her, broken like a flower, I felt
something akin to what a bird of prey feels,
when it knows that the dove will not escape.

And still I would not do an injustice to that
dove for any treasure on earth, for with love I
had in my heart at the same time an immense
compassion. A wonderful thing however: not-
withstandɪng my feeling for Lillian, the whole
day passed for us as if in mutual offence, or at
least in perplexity. I was racking my head to
discover how I could be alone even for a moment with her, but could not discover. Fortu-
nately Aunt Atkins came to my aid ; she declared
that the little one needed more exercise, that
confinement in the stifling wagon was injuring
her health. I fell upon the thought that she
ought to ride on horseback, and ordered
Simpson to saddle a horse for her ; and though
there were no side-saddles in the train, one of
those Mexɪcan saddles with a high pommel
which women use everywhere on the frontier
prairies, could serve her very well. I forbade
Lillian to loiter behind far enough to drop out
of view. To be lost in the open prairie was
rather difficult, because people, whom I sent

out for game, circled about a considerable
distance in every direction. There was no
danger from the Indians, for that part of the
prairie, as far as the Winnebago, was visited by
the Pawnees only during the great hunts, which
had not begun yet. But the southern forest-
tract abounded in wild beasts, not all of which
were grass eating; wariness, therefore, was far
from superfluous.

To tell the truth I thought that Lillian
would keep near me for safety; this would permit us to be alone rather frequently. Usually
I pushed forward in time of march some distance, having before me only the two half-
breed scouts, and behind the whole caravan.
So it happened in fact, and I was at once inex-
pressibly and truly happy, the first day, when I
saw my sweet Amazon moving forward at a
light gallop from the direction of the train.
The movement of the horse unwound her
tresses somewhat, and care for her skirt, which
was the least trifle short for the saddle, had

painted her face with a charming anxiety. When she came up she was like a rose; for she knew that she was going into a trap laid by me so that we might be alone with each other, and knowing this she came, though blushing, and as if unwilling, feigning that she knew nothing. My heart beat as if I had been a young student; and, when our horses were abreast, I was angry with myself, because I knew not what to say. At the same time such sweet and powerful desires began to go between us, that I, urged by some unseen power, bent toward Lillian as if to straighten something in the mane of her horse, and meanwhile I pressed my lips to her hand, which was resting on the pommel of the saddle. A certain unknown and unspeakable happiness, greater and keener than all delights that I had known in life till that moment, passed through my bones. I pressed that little hand to my heart and began to tell Lillian, that if God had bestowed all the kingdoms of the earth on me, and all the treasures in existence. I would not give for anything one tress of her hair, for she had taken me soul and body forever.

"Lillian, Lillian," said I further, "I will never leave you. I will follow you through mountains and deserts, I will kiss your feet and I will pray to you; only love me a little, only tell me that in your heart I mean something."

Thus speaking, I thought that my bosom would burst, when she, with the greatest confusion, began to repeat, —

"O Ralph! you know well! you know everything!"

I did not know just this, whether to laugh or to cry, whether to run away or to remain; and, as I hope for salvation to-day, I felt saved then, for nothing in the world was lacking to me.

Thenceforth so far as my occupations permitted, we were always together. And those occupations decreased every day till we reached the Missouri. Perhaps no caravan had more success than ours during the first

month of the journey. Men and animals were
growing accustomed to order and skilled in
travelling; hence I had less need to look
after them, while the confidence which the
people gave me upheld perfect order in the
train. Besides, abundance of provisions and
the fine spring weather roused joyfulness and
increased good health. I convinced myself
daily, that my bold plan of conducting the
caravan not by the usual route through
St. Louis and Kansas, but through Iowa and
Nebraska, was best. There heat almost unendurable tortured people, and in the un-
healthy region between the Mississippi and
Missouri fevers and other diseases thinned
the ranks of emigrants; here, by reason of
the cooler climate, cases of weakness were
fewer, and our labor was less.

It is true that the road by St. Louis was in
the earlier part of it freer from Indians; but my
train, composed of two or three hundred men
well furnished with weapons and ready for fight-

ing, had no cause to fear wild tribes, especially
those inhabiting Iowa, who though meeting
white men oftener, and, having more frequent
experience of what their hands could do, had
not the courage to rush at large parties. It
was only needful to guard against stampedes, or
night attacks on mules and horses, — the loss
of draught-animals puts a caravan on the prairies in a terrible position.   But against that there
was diligence and the experience of sentries who,
for the greater part, were as well acquainted
with the stratagems of Indians as I was.

When once I had introduced travelling discipline and made men accustomed to it, I had
incomparably less to do during the day, and
could devote more time to the feelings which
had seized my heart. In the evening I went
to sleep with the thought: "To-morrow I
shall see Lillian;" in the morning I said to
myself: "To-day I shall see Lillian;" and every
day I was happier and every day more in love.
In the caravan people began by degrees to

notice this; but no one took it ill of me, for Lillian and I possessed the good-will of those people. Once old Smith said in passing: " God bless you, captain, and you, Lillian." That connecting of our names made us happy all day. Aunt Grosvenor and Aunt Atkins whispered something frequently in Lillian's ear, which made her blush like the dawn, but she would never tell me what it was. Henry Simpson looked on us rather gloomily, — perhaps he was forging some plan in his soul, but I paid no heed to that.

Every morning at four I was at the head of the caravan; before me the scouts, some fifteen hundred yards distant, sang songs, which their Indian mothers had taught them; behind me at the same distance moved the caravan, like a white ribbon on the prairie, — and what a wonderful moment, when, about two hours later, I hear on a sudden behind me the tramp of a horse. I look, and behold the sight of my soul, my beloved is approaching.

The morning breeze bears behind her her hair, which either had been loosened from the movement, or badly fastened on purpose, for the little rogue knew that she looked better that way, that I liked her that way, and that when the wind threw the tress on me I pressed it to my lips. I feign not to notice her tricks, and in this agreeable meeting the morning begins for us. I taught her the Polish phrase : " Dzien dobry " (good morning). When I heard her pronouncing those words, she seemed still dearer; the memory of my country, of my family, of years gone by, of that which had been, of that which had passed, flew before my eyes on that prairie like mews of the ocean. More than once I would have broken out in weeping, but from shame I restrained with my eyelids the tears that were ready to flow. She, seeing that the heart was melting in me, repeated like a trained starling : " Dzien dobry ! dzien dobry ! dzien dobry ! " And how was I not to love my starling beyond everything? I taught her then

other phrases; and when her lips struggled
with our difficult sounds, and I laughed at a
faulty pronunciation, she pouted like a little
child, feigning anger and resentment. But we
had no quarrels, and once only a cloud flew
between us. One morning I pretended to
tighten a strap on her stirrup, but in truth the
leopard Uhlan was roused in me, and I began to
kiss her foot, or rather the poor shoe worn out
in the wilderness. Then she drew her foot
close to the horse, and repeating: "No, Ralph!
no! no!" sprang to one side; and though I
implored and strove to pacify her she would
not come near me. She did not return to
the caravan, however, fearing to pain me too
much. I feigned a sorrow a hundred times
greater than I felt in reality, and sinking into
silence, rode on as if all things had ended on
earth for me. I knew that compassion would
stir in her, as indeed it did; for soon, alarmed
at my silence, she began to ride up at one side
and look at my eyes, like a child which wants

to know if its mother is angry yet, — and I, wishing to preserve a gloomy visage, had to turn aside to avoid laughing aloud.

But this was one time only. Usually we were as gladsome as prairie squirrels, and sometimes, God forgive me, I, the leader of that caravan, became a child with her. More than once when we were riding side by side I would turn on a sudden, saying to her that I had something important and new to tell, and when she held her inquisitive ear I whispered into it: "I love." Then she also whispered into my ear in answer, with a smile and blush, "I also!" And thus we confided our secrets to each other on the prairie, where the wind alone could overhear us.

In this manner day shot after day so quickly, that, as I thought, the morning seemed to touch the evening like links in a chain. At times some event of the journey would vary such pleasant monotony. A certain Sunday the halfbreed Wichita caught with a lasso an antelope

of a large kind, and with her a fawn which I
gave to Lillian, who made for it a collar on which
was put a bell, taken from a mule. This fawn
we called Katty. In a week it was tame, and ate
from our hands. During the march I would
ride on one side of Lillian, and Katty would
run on the other, raising its great black eyes
and begging with a bleat for caresses.

Beyond the Winnebago we came out on a
plain as level as a table, broad, rich, primeval.
The scouts vanished from our eyes at times in
the grass; our horses waded, as if in a river. I
showed Lillian that world altogether new to her,
and when she was delighted with its beauties, I
felt proud that that kingdom of mine was so
pleasing to her. It was spring, — April was
barely reaching its end, the time of richest
growth for grasses of all sorts. What was to
bloom on the plains was blooming already.

In the evening such intoxicating odors came
from the prairie, as from a thousand censers;
in the day, when the wind blew and shook the

flowery expanse, the eye was just pained with the glitter of red, blue, yellow, and colors of all kinds. From the dense bed shot up the slender stalks of yellow flowers, like our mullein; around these wound the silver threads of a plant called "tears," whose clusters, composed of transparent little balls, are really like tears. My eyes, used to reading in the prairie, discovered repeatedly plants that I knew: now it was the large-leaved kalumna, which cures wounds; now the plant called "white and red stockings," which closes its cups at the approach of man or beast; finally, "Indian hatchets," the odor of which brings sleep and almost takes away consciousness. I taught Lillian at that time to read in this Divine book, saying, —

"It will come to you to live in forests and on plains; it is well then to know them in season."

In places on the level prairie rose, as if they were oases, groups of cottonwood or alder, so

wreathed with wild grapes and lianas that they
could not be recognized under the tendrils and
leaves. On the lianas in turn climbed ivy
and the prickly, thorny "wachtia," resembling
wild roses. Flowers were just dropping at all
points; inside, underneath that screen and
beyond that wall, was a certain mysterious
gloom; at the tree trunks were sleeping great
pools of water of the spring-time, which the
sun was unable to drink up; from the tree-
tops and among the brocade of flowers came
wonderful voices and the calling of birds.
When for the first time I showed such trees
to Lillian and such hanging cascades of flowers, she stood as if fixed to the earth, repeating with clasped hands, —

"Oh, Ralph! is that real?"

She said that she was a little afraid to enter
such a depth; but one afternoon, when the
heat was great, and over the prairie was flying,
as it were, the hot breath of the Texan wind,
we rode in, and Katty came after us.

We stopped at a little pool, which reflected
our two horses and our two forms; we remained in silence for a time. It was cool
there, obscure, solemn as in a Gothic cathe-
dral, and somewhat awe-inspiring. The light
of day came in bedimmed, greenish from the
leaves. Some bird, hidden under the cupola
of lianas, cried, "No! no! no!" as if warn-
ing us not to go farther; Katty began to
tremble and nestle up to the horses; Lillian
and I looked at each other suddenly, and for
the first time our lips met, and having met
could not separate. She drank my soul, I
drank her soul. Breath began to fail each
of us, still lips were on lips. At last her eyes
were covered with mist, and the hands which
she had placed on my shoulders were trembling
as in a fever: she was seized with a kind of
oblivion of her own existence, so that she grew
faint and placed her head on my bosom. We
were drunk with each other, with bliss, and
with ecstasy. I dared not move; but because

I had a soul overfilled, because I loved a hundred times more than may be thought or expressed, I raised my eyes to discover if through the thick leaves I could see the sky.

Recovering our senses, we came out at last from beneath the green density to the open prairie, where we were surrounded by the bright sunshine and warm breeze; before us was spread the broad and gladsome landscape. Prairie chickens were fluttering in the grass, and on slight elevations, which were perforated like a sieve by prairie dogs, stood, as it were, an army of those little creatures, which vanished under the earth at our coming; directly in front was the caravan, and horsemen careering around it.

It seemed to me that we had come out of a dark chamber to the white world, and the same thought must have come to Lillian. The brightness of the day rejoiced me; but that excess of golden light and the memory of rapturous kisses. traces of which were still evident

on her face, penetrated Lillian as it were with
alarm and with sadness.

"Ralph, will you not take that ill of me?"
asked she, on a sudden.

"What comes to your head, O my own!
God forget me if in my heart there is any feeling but respect and the highest love for you."

"I did that because I love greatly," said she;
and therewith her lips began to quiver and
she wept in silence, and though I was working
the soul out of myself she remained sad all that
day.

CHAPTER IV

At last we came to the Missouri. Indians chose generally the time of crossing that river to fall upon caravans; defence is most difficult when some wagons are on one bank, and some in the river; when the draught-beasts are stubborn and balky, and disorder rises among the people. Indeed, I noticed, before our arrival at the river, that Indian spies had for two days been following us; I took every precaution therefore, and led the train in complete military order. I did not permit wagons to

loiter on the prairie, as in the eastern districts
of Iowa ; the men had to stay together and be
in perfect readiness for battle.

When we had come to the bank and found
a ford, I ordered two divisions, of sixty men
each, to intrench themselves on both banks,
so as to secure the passage under cover
of small forts and the muzzles of rifles. The
remaining hundred and twenty emigrants had
to take the train over. I did not send in
more than a few wagons at once, so as to avoid
confusion. With such an arrangement everything took place in the greatest order, and
attack became impossible, for the attackers
would have had to carry one or the other
intrenchment before they could fall upon those
who were crossing the river.

How far these precautions were not superfluous the future made evident, for two years
later four hundred Germans were cut to pieces
by the Kiowas, at the place where Omaha
stands at this moment.   I had this advan-

tage besides: my men, who previously had
heard more than once narratives, which went
to the East, of the terrible danger of crossing the yellow waters of the Missouri, seeing the firmness and ease with which I had
solved the problem, gained blind confidence,
and began to look on me as some ruling
spirit of the plains.

Daily did those praises and that enthusiasm
reach Lillian, in whose loving eyes I grew to be
a legendary hero. Aunt Atkins said to her:
" While your Pole is with you, you may sleep
out in the rain, for he won't let the drops fall
on you." And the heart rose in my maiden
from those praises. During the whole time of
crossing I could give her hardly a moment,
and could only say hurriedly with my eyes
what my lips could not utter. All day I was
on horseback, now on one bank, now on the
other, now in the water. I was in a hurry to
advance as soon as possible from those thick
yellow waters, which were bearing down with

them rotten trees, bunches of leaves, grass, and malodorous mud from Dakota, infectious with fever.

Besides this, the people were wearied immensely, from continual watching; the horses grew sick from unwholesome water, which we could not use until we had kept it in charcoal a number of hours.

At last, after eight days' time, we found ourselves on the right bank of the river without having broken a wagon, and with the loss of only seven head of mules and horses. That day, however, the first arrows fell, for my men killed, and afterward, according to the repulsive habit of the plains, scalped three Indians, who had been trying to push in among the mules. In consequence of this deed an embassy of six leading warriors of the Bloody Tracks, belonging to the Pawnee stock, visited us on the following day. They sat down at our fire with tremendous importance, demanding horses and mules in return for the dead men. declaring that, in case of refusal, five hundred warriors would attack us immediately. I made no great account of those five hundred warriors, since I had the train in order and defended with in-trenchments. I saw well that that embassy had been sent merely because those wild people had caught at the first opportunity to extort some-thing without an attack, in the success of which they had lost faith. I should have driven them away in one moment, had I not wished to exhibit them to Lillian. In fact, while they were sitting at the council-fire motionless, with eyes fixed on the flame, she, concealed in the wagon, was looking with alarm and curiosity at their dress trimmed at the seams with human hair, their tomahawks adorned with feathers on the handles, and at their faces painted black and red, which meant war. In spite of these pre-parations, however, I refused their demand sharply, and, passing from a defensive to an offensive rôle, declared that if even one mule disappeared from the train, I would go to their

5

tribe myself and scatter the bones of their five hundred warriors over the prairie.

They went away, repressing their rage with difficulty, but when going they brandished their tomahawks over their heads in sign of war. However, my words sank in their memory; for at the time of their departure two hundred of my men, prepared purposely, rose up with threatening aspect, rattling their weapons, and gave forth a shout of battle. That readiness made a deep impression on the wild warriors.

Some hours later Henry Simpson, who at his own instance had gone out to observe the embassy, returned, all panting, with news that a considerable division of Indians was approaching us.

I, knowing Indian ways perfectly, knew that those were mere threats, for the Indians, armed with bows made of hickory, were not in numbers sufficient to meet Kentucky rifles of long range. I said that to Lillian, wishing to quiet her, for she was trembling like a leaf; but all the others were sure that a battle was coming; the younger ones, whose warlike spirit was roused, wished for it eagerly.

In fact, we heard the howling of the red-skins soon after; still, they kept at the distance of some gun-shots, as if seeking a favorable moment.

In our camp immense fires, replenished with cottonwood and willows, were burning all night; the men stood guard around the wagons; the women were singing psalms from fear; the mules, not driven out as usual to the night pasture, but confined behind the wagons, were braying and biting one another; the dogs, feeling the nearness of the Indians, were howling, — in a word, it was noisy and threatening throughout the camp. In brief moments of silence we heard the mournful and ominous howling of the Indian outposts, calling with the voices of coyotes.

About midnight the Indians tried to set fire to the prairie, but the damp grass of spring would not burn, though for some days not a rain-drop had fallen on that region.

When riding around the camp-ground before daybreak I had a chance of seeing Lillian for a moment. I found her sleeping from weariness, with her head resting on the knees of Aunt Atkins, who, armed with a bowie-knife, had sworn to destroy the whole tribe, if one of them dared to come near her darling. As to me, I looked on that fair sleeping face with the love not only of a man, but almost of a mother, and I felt equally with Aunt Atkins that I would tear into pieces any one who would threaten my beloved. In her was my joy, in her my delight; beyond her I had nothing but endless wander-ing, tramping, and mishaps. Before my eyes I had the best proof of this: in the distance were the prairie, the rattle of weapons, the night on horseback, the struggle with predatory redskin murderers; nearer, right there before my face, was the quiet sleep of that dear one, so full of faith and trust in me, that my word alone had convinced her that there could be no attack, and she had fallen asleep as full of confidence as if under her father's roof.

When I looked at those two pictures, I felt for the first time how that adventurous life without a morrow had wearied me, and I saw at once that I should find rest and satisfaction with her alone. "If only to California!" thought I, "if only to California! But the toils of the journey — merely one-half of which, and that half the easiest, is over — are evident already on that pallid face; but a beautiful rich country is waiting for us there, with its warm sky and eternal spring." Thus meditating, I covered the feet of the sleeper with my buffalo-robe, so that the night cold might not harm her, and returned to the end of the camp.

It was time, for a thick mist had begun to rise from the river; the Indians might really take advantage of it and try their fortune. The fires were dimmed more and more, and grew pale. An hour later one man could not see another if

ten paces distant. I gave command then to cry
on the square every minute, and soon nothing
was heard in that camp but the prolonged
"All 's well !" which passed from mouth to
mouth like the words of a litany.

But the Indian camp had grown perfectly
still, as if its occupants were dumb. This began to alarm me. At the first dawn an immense
weariness mastered us ; God knows how many
nights the majority of the men had passed
without sleep, — besides, the fog, wonderfully
penetrating, sent a chill and a shiver through
all.

Would it not be better, thought I, instead of
standing on one place and waiting for what may
please the Indians, to attack and scatter them
to the four winds? This was not simply the
whim of an Uhlan, but an absolute need ; for a
daring and lucky attack might gain us great
glory, which, spreading among the wild tribes,
would give us safety for a long stretch of road.

Leaving behind me one hundred and thirty

men, under the lead of the old prairie wolf, Smith, I commanded a hundred others to mount their horses, and we moved forward somewhat cautiously, but gladly, for the cold had become more annoying, and in this way it was possible to warm ourselves at least. At twice the distance of a gunshot we raced forward at a gallop with shouting, and in the midst of a musket-fire rushed, like a storm, on the savages. A ball, sent from our side by some awkward marksman, whistled right at my ear, but only tore my cap.

Meanwhile, we were on the necks of the Indians, who expected anything rather than an attack, for this was surely the first time that emigrants had charged the besiegers. Great alarm so blinded them, therefore, that they fled in every direction, howling from fright like wild beasts, and perishing without resistance. A smaller division of these people, pushed to the river and, deprived of retreat, defended themselves so sternly and stubbornly that they chose to rush into the water rather than beg for life.

Their spears pointed with sharpened deer-horns and tomahawks made of hard flint were not very dangerous, but they used them with wonderful skill. We burst through these, however, in the twinkling of an eye. I took one prisoner, a sturdy rascal, whose hatchet and arm I broke in the moment of fighting with hatchets.

We seized a few tens of horses, but so wild and vicious that there was no use in them. We made a few prisoners, all wounded. I gave command to care for these most attentively, and set them free afterward at Lillian's request, having given them blankets, arms, and horses, necessary for men seriously wounded. These poor fellows, believing that we would tie them to stakes for torture, had begun to chant their monotonous death-songs, and were simply terrified at first by what had happened. They thought that we would liberate only to hunt

them in Indian fashion; but seeing that no
danger threatened, they went away, exalting our
bravery and the goodness of "Pale Flower,"
which name they had given Lillian.

That day ended, however, with a sad event,
which cast a shade on our delight at such a considerable victory, and its foreseen results. Among
my men there were none killed; a number,
nevertheless, had received wounds more or less
serious; the most grievously wounded was
Henry Simpson, whose eagerness had borne
him away during battle. In the evening his
condition grew so much worse, that he was
dying; he wished to make some confession to
me, but, poor fellow, he could not speak, for
his jaw had been broken by a tomahawk. He
merely muttered: "Pardon, my captain!"
Immediately convulsions seized him. I divined
what he wanted, remembering the bullet which
in the morning had whistled at my ear, and I
forgave him, as becomes a Christian. I knew
that he carried with him to the grave a deep,

though unacknowledged feeling for Lillian, and supposed that he might have sought death.

He died about midnight ; we buried him under an immense cottonwood, on the bark of which I carved out a cross with my knife.

CHAPTER V.

ON the following day we moved on. Before us was a prairie still more extensive, more level, wilder, a region which the foot of a white man had hardly touched at that time, — in a word, we were in Nebraska.

During the first days we moved quickly enough over treeless expanses, but not without difficulty, for there was an utter lack of wood for fuel. The banks of the Platte River, which cuts the whole length of those measureless plains, were, it is true, covered with a dense growth of

osier and willow; but that river having a shallow
bed, had overflowed, as is usual in spring, and
we had to keep far away.   Meanwhile we passed
the nights at smouldering fires of buffalo dung,
which, not dried yet sufficiently by the sun, rather
smouldered with a blue flame than burnt.   We
hurried on then with every effort toward Big Blue
River, where we could find abundance of fuel.

The country around us bore every mark of a
primitive land.   Time after time, before the
train, which extended now in a very loose line,
rushed herds of antelopes with ruddy hair and
with white under the belly; at times there appeared in the waves of grass the immense
shaggy heads of buffaloes, with bloodshot eyes
and steaming nostrils; then again these beasts
were seen in crowds, like black moving patches
on the distant prairie.

In places we passed near whole towns formed
of mounds raised by prairie dogs.   The Indians
did not show themselves at first, and only a number of days later did we see three wild horsemen,

ornamented with feathers; but they vanished before our eyes in an instant, like phantoms. I convinced myself afterward that the bloody lesson which I had given them on the Missouri, made the name of "Big Ara" (for thus they had modified Big Ralph) terrible among the many tribes of prairie robbers; the kindness shown the prisoners had captivated those people, wild and revengeful, though not devoid of knightly feeling.

When we had come to Big Blue River, I resolved to halt ten days at its woody banks. The second half of the road, which lay before us, was more difficult than the first, for beyond the prairie were the Rocky Mountains, and farther on the "Bad Lands" of Utah and Nevada. Meanwhile, our mules and horses, in spite of abundant pasture, had become lean and road-weary; hence it was needful to recruit their strength with a considerable rest. For this purpose we halted in the triangle formed by the Big Blue River and Beaver Creek.

It was a strong position, which, secured on two sides by the rivers and on the third by the wagons, had become almost impregnable, especially since wood and water were found on the spot. Of camp labor there was scarcely any, excessive watching was not needed, and the emigrants could use their leisure with perfect freedom. The days, too, were the most beautiful of our journey. The weather continued to be marvellous, and the nights grew so warm that one might sleep in the open air.

The people went out in the morning to hunt, and returned at midday, weighed down with antelopes and prairie birds, which lived in millions in the country about; the rest of the day they spent eating, sleeping, singing, or shooting for amusement at wild geese, which flew in whole flocks above the camp.

In my life there has never been anything better or happier than those ten days between the rivers. From morning till evening I did not part from Lillian, and that beginning not of passing visits, but, as it were, of life, convinced me more and more that I had loved once and forever her, the mild and gentle. I became acquainted with Lillian in those days more nearly and more deeply. At night, instead of sleeping, I thought frequently of what she was, and that she had become to me as dear and as needful in life as air is for breathing. God sees that I loved greatly her beautiful face, her long tresses, and her eyes, — as blue as that sky bending over Nebraska, — and her form, lithe and slender, which seemed to say: "Support and defend me forever; without thee I cannot help myself in the world!" God sees that I loved everything that was in her, every poor bit of clothing of hers, and she attracted me with such force that I could not resist; but there was another charm in her for me, and that was her sweetness and sensitiveness.

Many women have I met in life, but never have I met and never shall I meet another such.

and I feel endless grief when I think of her. The soul in Lillian Morris was as sensitive as that flower whose leaves nestle in when you draw near to it. Sensitive to every word of mine, she comprehended everything and reflected every thought, just as deep, transparent water reflects all that passes by the brink of it. At the same time that pure heart yielded itself to feeling with such timidity that I felt how great her love must be when she weakened and gave herself in sacrifice. And then everything honorable in my soul was changed into one feeling of gratitude to her. She was simply my one, my dearest in the world; so modest, that I had to persuade her that to love is not a sin, and I was breaking my head continually over this: how can I persuade her? In such emotions time passed for us at the meeting of the rivers, till at last my supreme happiness was accomplished.

One morning at daybreak we started to walk up Beaver Creek; I wanted to show her the

beavers; a whole kingdom of them was flour-
ishing not farther than half a mile from our
wagons. Walking along the bank carefully, near
the bushes, we came soon to our object. There
was a little bay as it were, or a lakelet, formed
by the creek, at the brink of which stood two
great hickory-trees; at the very bank grew
weeping-willows, half their branches in the
water. The beaver-dam, a little higher up in
the creek, stopped its flow, and kept the water
ever at one height in the lakelet, above whose
clear surface rose the round cupola-shaped
houses of these very clever animals.

Probably the foot of man had never stood
before in that retreat, hidden on all sides by
trees. Pushing apart cautiously the slender
limbs of the willows, we looked at the water,
which was as smooth as a mirror, and blue.
The beavers were not at their work yet; the
little water-town slumbered in visible quiet;
and such silence reigned on the lake that I
heard Lillian's breath when she thrust her

6

golden head through the opening in the branches with mine and our temples touched. I caught her waist with my arm to hold her on the slope of the bank, and we waited patiently, delighted with what our eyes were taking in.

Accustomed to life in wild places, I loved Nature as my own mother, though simply; but I felt that something like God's delight in Creation was present.

It was early morning; the light had barely come, and was reddening among the branches of the hickories; the dew was dropping from the leaves of the willows, and the world was growing brighter each instant. Later on, there came to the other shore prairie chickens, gray, with black throats, pretty crests on their heads, and they drank water, raising their bills as they swallowed.

"Ah, Ralph! how good it is here," whispered Lillian.

There was nothing in my head then but a

cottage in some lonely canyon, she with me, and such a rosary of peaceful days, flowing calmly into eternity and endless rest. It seemed to us that we had brought to that wedding of Nature our own wedding, to that calm our calm, and to that bright light the bright light of happiness within us.

Now the smooth surface described itself in a circle, and from the water came up slowly the bearded face of a beaver, wet and rosy from the gleam of the morning; then a second, and the two little beasts swam toward the lake, pushing apart with their noses blue lines, puffing and muttering. They climbed the dam, and, sitting on their haunches, began to call; at that signal heads, larger and smaller, rose up as if by enchantment; a plashing was heard in the lake. The herd appeared at first to be playing, — simply diving and screaming in its own fashion from delight; but the first pair, looking from the dam, gave a sudden, prolonged whistle from their nostrils, and in a twinkle half of the beavers were on the dam, and the other half had swum to the banks and vanished under the willows, where the water began to boil, and a sound as it were of sawing indicated that the little beasts were working there, cutting branches and bark.

Lillian and I looked long, very long, at these acts, and at the pleasures of animal life until man disturbs it. Wishing to change her position, she moved a branch accidentally, and in the twinkle of an eye every beaver had vanished; only the disturbed water indicated that something was beneath; but after a while the water became smooth, and silence surrounded us again, interrupted only by the woodpeckers striking the firm bark of the hickories.

Meanwhile the sun had risen above the trees and began to heat powerfully. Since Lillian did not feel tired yet, we resolved to go around the little lake. On the way we came to a small stream which intersected the wood

and fell into the lake from the opposite side.
Lillian could not cross it, so I had to carry
her; and despite her resistance, I took her like
a child in my arms and walked into the water.
But that stream was a stream of temptations.
Fear lest I should fall made her seize my
neck with both arms, hold to me with all her
strength, and hide her shamed face behind my
shoulder; but I began straightway to press my
lips to her temple, whispering: " Lillian ! my
Lillian !" And in that way I carried her over
the water.

When I reached the other bank I wished
to carry her farther, but she tore herself from
me almost rudely. A certain disquiet seized
both of us; she began to look around as if
in fear, and now pallor and now ruddiness
struck her face in turn. We went on. I took
her hand and pressed it to my heart. At moments fear of myself seized me. The day
became sultry; heat flowed down from the sky
to the earth; the wind was not blowing, the

leaves on the hickories hung motionless, the
only sound was from woodpeckers striking the
bark as before; all seemed to be growing lan-
guid from heat and falling asleep. I thought
that some enchantment was in the air, in that
forest, and then I thought only that Lillian was
with me and that we were alone.

Meanwhile weariness began to come on
Lillian; her breathing grew shorter and more
audible, and on her face, usually pale, fiery
blushes beat forth. I asked if she was not
tired, and if she would not rest.

"Oh, no, no!" answered she quickly, as
if defending herself from even the thought;
but after a few tens of steps she tottered
suddenly and whispered, —

"I cannot, indeed, I cannot go farther."

Then I took her again in my arms and carried that dear burden to the edge of the shore,
where willows, hanging to the ground, formed
a shady corridor. In this green alcove I placed
her on the moss. I knelt down : and when I

looked at her the heart in me was straitened.
Her face was as pale as linen, and her staring
eyes looked on me with fear.

"Lillian, what is the matter?" cried I. "I
am with you." I bent to her feet then and covered them with kisses. "Lillian!" continued
I, "my only, my chosen, my wife!"

When I said these last words a shiver passed
through her from head to foot; and suddenly
she threw her arms around my neck with a
certain unusual power, as in a fever repeating, "My dear! my dear! my husband!"
Everything vanished from my eyes then, and
it seemed to me that the whole globe of the
earth was flying away with us.

I know not to this day how it could be that
when I recovered from that intoxication and
came to my senses twilight was shining again
among the dark branches of the hickories, but
it was the twilight of evening. The woodpeckers had ceased to strike the trees; one
twilight on the bottom of the lake was smiling

at that other which was in the sky; the inhabitants of the water had gone to sleep; the evening was beautiful, calm, filled with a red light; it was time to return to the camp.

When we had come out from beneath the weeping-willows, I looked at Lillian; there was not on her face either sadness or disquiet; in her upturned eyes was the light of calm resignation and, as it were, a bright aureole of sacrifice and dignity encircled her blessed head. When I gave her my hand, she inclined her head quietly to my shoulder, and, without turning her eyes from the heavens, she said to me:

"Ralph, repeat to me that I am your wife, and repeat it to me often."

Since there was neither in the deserts, nor in the place to which we were going, any marriage save that of hearts, I knelt down, and when she had knelt at my side, I said: "Before God, earth, and heaven, I declare to thee, Lillian Morris, that I take thee as wife. Amen."

To this she answered: "Now I am thine forever and till death, thy wife, Ralph!"

From that moment we were married ; she was not my sweetheart, she was my lawful wife. That thought was pleasant to both of us, — and pleasant to me, for in my heart there rose a new feeling of a certain sacred respect for Lillian, and for myself, a certain honorableness and great dignity through which love became ennobled and blessed. Hand in hand, with heads erect and confident look, we returned to the camp, where the people were greatly alarmed about us. A number of tens of men had gone out in every direction to look for us ; and with astonishment I learned afterward that some had passed around the lake, but could not discover us ; we on our part had not heard their shouts.

I summoned the people, and when they had assembled in a circle, I took Lillian by the hand, went into the centre of the circle, and said, —

"Gentlemen, be witnesses, that in your presence I call this woman, who stands with me, my wife; and bear witness of this before justice, before law, and before every one whosoever may ask you, either in the East or the West."

"We will! and hurrah for you both!" answered the miners.

Old Smith asked Lillian then, according to custom, if she agreed to take me as husband, and when she said "Yes," we were legally married before the people.

In the distant prairies of the West, and on all the frontiers where there are no towns, magistrates, or churches, marriages are not performed otherwise; and to this hour, if a man calls a woman with whom he lives under the same roof his wife, this declaration takes the place of all legal documents. No one of my men therefore wondered, or looked at my marriage otherwise than with the respect shown to custom; on the contrary, all were rejoiced, for, though I had held them more sternly than other leaders, they knew that I

did so honestly, and with each day they
showed me more good will, and my wife
was always the eye in the head of the caravan. Hence there began a holiday and amuse-
ments. The fires were stirred up; the Scots
took from their wagons the pipes, whose music
we both liked, since it was for us a pleasant
reminiscence; the Americans took out their
favorite ox-bones, and amid songs, shouts, and
shooting, the wedding evening passed for us.

Aunt Atkins embraced Lillian every little
while, now laughing, now weeping, now lighting her pipe, which went out the next moment. But I was touched most by the following ceremony which is a custom in that movable portion of the American population which
spends the greater part of its life in wagons.
When the moon went down the men fastened on the ramrods of their guns branches of
lighted osier, and a whole procession, under the
lead of old Smith, conducted us from wagon
to wagon, asking Lillian at each of them,

"Is this your home?" My beautiful love answered, "No!" and we went on. At Aunt Atkins' wagon a real tenderness took possession of us all, for in that one Lillian had ridden hitherto. When she said there also in a low voice, "No," Aunt Atkins bellowed like a buffalo, and seizing Lillian in her embrace, began to repeat: "My little one! my sweet!" sobbing meanwhile, and carried away with weeping. Lillian sobbed too; and then all those hardened hearts grew tender for an instant, and there was no eye to which tears did not come.

When we approached it, I barely recognized my wagon, it was decked with branches and flowers. Here the men raised the burning torches aloft, and Smith inquired in a louder and more solemn voice, —

"Is this your home?"

"That's it! That's it!" answered Lillian.

Then all uncovered their heads, and there was such silence that I heard the hissing of the fire and the sound of the burnt twigs falling on the ground; the old white-haired miner, stretching out his sinewy hands over us, said, —

"May God bless you both, and your house, Amen!"

A triple hurrah answered that blessing. All separated then, leaving me and my loved one alone.

When the last man had gone, she rested her head on my breast, whispering: "Forever! forever!" and at that moment the stars in our souls outnumbered the stars of the sky.

CHAPTER VI

NEXT morning early I left my wife sleeping and went to find flowers for her. While looking for them, I said to myself every moment: "You are married!" and the thought filled me with such delight, that I raised my eyes to the Lord of Hosts, thanking Him for having permitted me to live to the time in which a man becomes himself genuinely and rounds out his life with the life of another loved beyond all. I had something now of my own in the world, and though that canvas-cov-

ered wagon was my only house and hearth, I
felt richer at once, and looked at my previous
wandering lot with pity, and with wonder that
I could have lived in that manner hitherto.
Formerly it had not even come to my head
what happiness there is in that word "wife," —
happiness which called to my heart's blood with
that name, and to the best part of my own
soul.   For a long time I had so loved Lillian
that I saw the whole world through her only,
connected everything with her, and understood
everything only as it related to her.   And now
when I said "wife," that meant, mine, mine
forever; and I thought that I should go wild
with delight, for it could not find place in my
head, that I, a poor man, should possess such
a treasure.   What then was lacking to me?
Nothing.   Had those prairies been warmer,
had there been safety there for her, had it not
been for the obligation to lead people to the
place to which I had promised to lead them,
I was ready not to go to California, but to settle

even in Nebraska, if with Lillian. I had been
going to California to dig gold, but now I was
ready to laugh at the idea. "What other
riches can I find there, when I have her?" I
asked myself. "What do we care for gold?
See, I will choose some canyon, where there is
spring all the year; I will cut down trees for a
house, and live with her, and a plough and a
gun will give us life. We shall not die of
hunger — " These were my thoughts while
gathering flowers, and when I had enough of
them I returned to the camp. On the road I
met Aunt Atkins.

"Is the little one sleeping?" asked she,
taking from her mouth for a moment the insep-
arable pipe.

"She is sleeping," answered I.

To this Aunt Atkins, blinking with one eye,
added, —

"Ah, you rascal!"

Meanwhile the "little one" was not sleeping, for we both saw her coming down from the

7

wagon, and shielding her eyes against the sunlight with her hand, she began to look on every
side. Seeing me, she ran up all rosy and fresh,
as the morning. When I opened my arms, she
fell into them panting, and putting up her
mouth, began to repeat : —

"Dzien dobry ! dzien dobry ! dzien dobry ! "

Then she stood on her toes, and looking into
my eyes, asked with a roguish smile, "Am I
your wife ? "

What was there to answer, except to kiss
without end and fondle ? And thus passed the
whole time at that meeting of rivers, for old
Smith had taken on himself all my duties till
the resumption of our journey.

We visited our beavers once more, and the
stream, through which I carried her now without
resistance. Once we went up Blue River in a
little redwood canoe. At a bend of the stream
I showed Lillian buffaloes near by, driving their
horns into the bank, from which their whole
heads were covered as if with armor of dried

clay. But two days before starting, these expeditions ceased, for first the Indians had appeared in the neighborhood, and second my dear lady had begun to be weak somewhat. She grew pale and lost strength, and when I inquired what the trouble was, she answered only with a smile and the assurance that it was nothing. I watched over her sleep, I nursed her as well as I was able, almost preventing the breezes from blowing on her, and grew thin from anxiety. Aunt Atkins blinked mysteriously with her left eye when talking of Lillian's illness, and sent forth such dense rolls of smoke that she grew invisible behind them. I was disturbed all the more, because sad thoughts came to Lillian at times. She had beaten it into her head that maybe it was not permitted to love so intensely as we were loving, and once, putting her finger on the Bible, which we read every day, she said sadly, —

" Read, Ralph."

I looked, and a certain wonderful feeling

seized my heart too, when I read, " Who
changed the truth of God into a lie, and worshipped and served the creature more than the
Creator, who is blessed forever." She said
when I had finished reading, " But if God is
angry at this, I know that with His goodness
He will punish only me."

I pacified her by saying that love was simply an angel, who flies from the souls of two
people to God and takes Him praise from the
earth. After that there was no talk between us
touching such things, since preparations for the
journey had begun. The fitting up of wagons
and beasts, and a thousand occupations, stole
my time from me. When at last the hour came
for departure we took tearful farewell of that
river fork, which had witnessed so much of our
happiness ; but when I saw the train stretching
out again on the prairie, the wagons one after
another and lines of mules before the wagons,
I felt a certain consolation at the thought that
the end of the journey would be nearer each

day, that a few months more and we should see California, toward which we were striving with such toil.

But the first days of the journey did not pass over-successfully. Beyond the Missouri, as far as the foot of the Rocky Mountains, the prairie rises continually over enormous expanses; therefore the beasts were easily wearied, and were often tired out. Besides, we could not approach the Platte River, for, though the flood had decreased, it was the time of the great spring hunts, and a multitude of Indians circled around the river, looking for herds of buffaloes moving northward. Night service became difficult and wearying; no night passed without alarms.

On the fourth day after we had moved from the river fork, I broke up a considerable party of Indian plunderers at the moment when they were trying to stampede our mules. But worst of all were the nights without fire. We were unable to approach the Platte River, and frequently had nothing to burn, and toward morning drizzling rain began to fall; buffalo dung, which in case of need took the place of wood, got wet, and would not burn.

The buffaloes filled me with alarm also. Sometimes we saw herds of some thousands on the horizon, rushing forward like a storm, crushing everything before them. Were such a herd to strike the train, we should perish every one without rescue. To complete the evil, the prairie was swarming at that time with beasts of prey of all species; after the buffaloes and Indians, came terrible gray bears, cougars, big wolves from Kansas and the Indian Territory. At the small streams, where we stopped sometimes for the night, we saw at sunset whole menageries coming to drink after the heat of the day. Once a bear rushed at Wichita, our half-breed; and if I had not run up, with Smith and the other scout, Tom, to help him, he would have been torn to pieces. I opened the head of the monster with an axe, which I brought down with such force that the handle of tough hickory was broken; still, the beast rushed at me once more, and fell only when Smith and Tom shot him in the ear from rifles. Those savage brutes were so bold that at night they came up to the very train; and in the course of a week we killed two not more than a hundred yards from the wagons. In consequence of this, the dogs raised such an uproar from twilight till dawn that it was impossible to close an eye.

Once I loved such a life; and when, a year before, I was in Arkansas, during the greatest heat, it was for me as in paradise. But now, when I remembered that in the wagon my beloved wife, instead of sleeping, was trembling about me, and ruining her health with anxiety, I wished all the Indians and bears and cougars in the lowest pit, and desired from my soul to secure as soon as possible the peace of that being so fragile, so delicate, and so worshipped, that I wished to bear her forever in my arms.

A great weight fell from my heart when, after three weeks of such crossings, I saw at last the waters of a river white as if traced out with chalk; this stream is called now Republican River, but at that time it had no name in English. Broad belts of dark willows, stretching like a mourning trail along the white waters, could afford us fuel in plenty; and though that kind of willow crackles in the fire, and shoots sparks with great noise, still it burns better than wet buffalo dung. I appointed at this place another rest of two days, because the rocks, scattered here and there by the banks of the river, indicated the proximity of a hilly country, difficult to cross, lying on both sides of the back of the Rocky Mountains. We were already on a considerable elevation above the sea, as could be known by the cold nights.

That inequality between day and night temperature troubled us greatly. Some people, among others old Smith, caught fevers, and had to go to their wagons. The seeds of the disease had clung to them, probably, at the unwholesome banks of the Missouri, and hardship caused the outbreak. The nearness of the mountains, however, gave hope of a speedy recovery; meanwhile, my wife nursed them with a devotion innate to gentle hearts only.

But she grew thin herself. More than once, when I woke in the morning, my first look fell on her beautiful face, and my heart beat uneasily at its pallor and the blue half circles under her eyes. It would happen that while I was looking at her in that way she would wake, smile at me, and fall asleep again. Then I felt that I would have given half my health of oak if we were in California; but California was still far, far away.

After two days we started again, and coming to the Republican River at noon, were soon moving along the fork of the White Man

toward the southern fork of the Platte, lying for
the most part in Colorado. The country became more mountainous at every step, and we
were really in the canyon along the banks of
which rose up in the distance higher and
higher granite cliffs, now standing alone, now
stretching out continuously like walls, now
closing more narrowly, now opening out on
both sides. Wood was not lacking, for all the
cracks and crannies of the cliffs were covered
with dwarf pine and dwarf oak as well. Here
and there springs were heard; along the rocky
walls scampered the wolverine. The air was
cool, pure, wholesome. After a week the fever ceased. But the mules and horses, forced
to eat food in which heather predominated,
instead of the juicy grass of Nebraska, grew
thinner and thinner, and groaned more loudly
as they pulled up the mountains our well filled
and weighty wagons.

At last on a certain afternoon we saw before
us beacons. as it were. or crested clouds half

melting in the distance, hazy, blue, azure, with white and gold on their crests, and immense in size, extending from the earth to the sky.

At this sight a shout rose in the whole caravan; men climbed to the tops of the wagons to see better, from every side thundered shouts: "Rocky Mountains! Rocky Mountains!" Caps were waving in the air, and on all faces enthusiasm was evident.

Thus the Americans greeted their Rocky Mountains, but I went to my wagon, and, pressing my wife to my breast, vowed faith to her once more in spirit before those heaven-touching altars, which expressed such solemn mysteriousness, majesty, unapproachableness, and immensity. The sun was just setting, and soon twilight covered the whole country; but those giants in the last rays seemed like measureless masses of burning coal and lava. Later on, that fiery redness passed into violet, ever darker, and at last all disappeared, and was merged into one darkness, through which gazed at us from above the stars, the twinkling eyes of the night.

But we were at least a hundred and fifty miles yet from the main chain; in fact, the mountains disappeared from our eyes next day, intercepted by cliffs; again they appeared and again they vanished, as our road went by turns.

We advanced slowly, for new obstacles stood in our way; and though we kept as much as possible to the bed of the river, frequently, where the banks were too steep, we had to go around and seek a passage by neighboring valleys. The ground in these valleys was covered with gray heather and wild peas, not good even for mules, and forming no little hindrance to the journey, for the long and powerful stems, twisting around, made it difficult to pass through them.

Sometimes we came upon openings and cracks in the earth, impassable and hundreds of yards long; these we had to go around also. Time after time the scouts, Wichıta and Tom, returned with accounts of new obstacles. The land bristled with rocks, or broke away suddenly.

On a certain day it seemed to us that we were going through a valley, when all at once the valley was missing; in place of it was a precipice so deep that the gaze went down with terror along the perpendicular wall, and the head became dizzy. Giant oaks, growing at the bottom of the abyss, seemed little black clumps, and the buffaloes pasturing among them like beetles. We entered more and more into the region of precipices, of stones, fragments, debris, and rocks thrown one on the other with a kind of wild disorder. The echo sent back twice and thrice from granite arches the curses of drivers and squealing of mules. On the prairie our wagons, rising high above the surface of the country, seemed lordly and immense; here before those perpendicular cliffs, the wagons became wonderfully small to the eye, and vanished in those gorges as if devoured by gigantic jaws. Little waterfalls, or as they are called by the Indians, " laughing waters," stopped the road to us every few hundred yards; toil exhausted our strength and that of the animals. Meanwhile, when at times the real chain of mountains appeared on the horizon, it seemed as far away and hazy as ever. Happily curiosity overcame in us even weariness, and the continual change of views kept it in practice. None of my people, not excepting those who were born in the Alleghanies, had ever seen such wild regions; I myself gazed with wonder on those canyons, along the edges of which the unbridled fancy of Nature had reared as it were castles, fortresses, and stone cities. From time to time we met Indians, but these were different from those on the prairies, very straggling and very much wilder.

The sight of white men roused in them
fear mingled with a desire for blood. They
seemed still more cruel than their brethren
in Nebraska; their stature was loftier, their
complexion much darker, their wide nostrils
and quick glances gave them the expression
of wild beasts caught in a trap. Their movements, too, had almost the quickness and
timidity of beasts. While speaking, they put
their thumbs to their cheeks, which were
painted in white and blue stripes. Their
weapons were tomahawks and bows, the latter
made of a certain kind of firm mountain
hawthorn, so rigid that my men could not
bend them. These savages, who in considerable numbers might have been very dangerous,
were distinguished by invincible thievishness;
happily they were few, the largest party that
we met not exceeding fifteen. They called
themselves Tabeguachis, Winemucas, and Yam-
pas. Our scout, Wichita, though expert in
Indian dialects, could not understand their

language; hence we could not make out in any way why all of them, pointing to the Rocky Mountains and then to us, closed and opened their palms, as if indicating some number.

The road became so difficult, that with the greatest exertion, we made barely fifteen miles a day. At the same time our horses began to die, being less enduring than mules and more choice of food; men failed in strength too, for during whole days they had to draw wagons with the mules, or to hold them in dangerous places. By degrees unwillingness seized the weakest; some got the rheumatism, and one, through whose mouth blood came from exertion, died in three days, cursing the hour in which it came to his head to leave New York. We were then in the worst part of the road, near the little river called by the Indians Kiowa. There were no cliffs there as high as on the Eastern boundary of Colorado; but the whole country, as far as

the eye could reach, was bristling with fragments thrown in disorder one upon another.
These fragments, some standing upright, others
overturned, presented the appearance of ruined
graveyards with fallen headstones. Those were
really the " Bad Lands " of Colorado, answering
to those which extended northward over Nebraska. With the greatest effort we escaped
from them in the course of a week.

CHAPTER VII.

At last we found ourselves at the foot of the
Rocky Mountains.

Fear seized me when I looked from a proxi-
mate point at that world of granite mountains,
whose sides were wrapped in mist, and whose
summits were lost somewhere in eternal snow
and clouds. Their size and silent majesty
pressed me to the earth; hence I bent before
the Lord, imploring Him to permit me to lead,
past those measureless walls, my wagons, my
people, and my wife. After such a prayer I

entered the stone gullies and corridors with more confidence. When they closed behind us we were cut off from the rest of the world. Above was the sky; in it a few eagles were screaming, around us was granite and then granite without end, — a genuine labyrinth of passages, vaults, ravines, openings, precipices, towers, silent edifices, and as it were chambers, gigantic and dreamy. There is such a solemnity there, and the soul is under such pressure, that a man knows not himself why he whispers instead of speaking aloud. It seems to him that the road is closing before him continually, that some voice is saying to him : " Go no farther, for there is no passage ! " It seems to him that he is attacking some secret on which God Himself has set a seal. At night, when those upright legions were standing as black as mourning, and the moon cast about their summits a silvery mantle of sadness, when certain wonderful shadows rose around the " laughing waters," a quiver passed through the most hardened adventurers. We spent whole hours by the fires, looking with a certain superstitious awe at the dark depths of the ravines, lighted by ruddy gleams; we seemed to think that something terrible might show itself any moment.

Once we found under a hollow in the cliff the skeleton of a man; and though from the remnant of the hair which had dried to the skull, we saw that he was an Indian, still an ominous feeling pressed our hearts, for that skeleton with grinning teeth seemed to forewarn us that whoso wandered in there would never come out again.

That same day the half-breed, Tom, was killed suddenly, having fallen with his horse from the edge of a cliff. A gloomy sadness seized the whole caravan; formerly we had advanced noisily and joyfully, now the drivers ceased to swear, and the caravan pushed forward in a silence broken only by the squeaking of wheels. The mules grew ill-tempered more frequently, and when one pair stood as still as if lashed to the earth, all the wagons behind them had to stop. I was most tortured by this, — that in those moments which were so difficult and oppressive, and in which my wife needed my presence more than at other times, I could not be near her ; for I had to double and treble myself almost, so as to give an example, uphold courage and confidence. The men, it is true, bore toil with the endurance innate with Americans, though they were simply using the last of their strength. But my health was proof against every hardship. There were nights in which I did not have two hours of sleep ; I dragged the wagons with others, I posted the sentries, I went around the square, — in a word, I performed service twice more burdensome than any one of the company ; but it is evident that happiness gave me strength. For when, wearied and beaten down, I came to my wagon, I found there everything that I held dearest : a faithful heart and a beloved hand, that wiped my wearied forehead. Lillian, though suffering a little, never went to sleep

wittingly before my arrival; and when I re-
proached her she closed my mouth with a kiss
and a prayer not to be angry. When I told her
to sleep she did so, holding my hand. Frequently in the night, when she woke, she covered me with beaver skins, so that I might rest
better. Always mild, sweet, loving, she cared
for me and brought me to worship her simply.
I kissed the hem of her garment, as if it had
been the most sacred thing, and that wagon of
ours became for me almost a church. That
little one in presence of those heaven-touching
walls of granite, upon which she cast her up-
raised eyes, covered them for me in such a way,
that in presence of her they vanished from before
me, and amid all those immensities I saw only
her. What is there wonderful, if when strength
failed others, I had strength still, and felt that so
long as it was a question of her I would never
fail?

After three weeks' journey we came at last to
a more spacious canyon formed by White River.

At the entrance to it the Winta Indians prepared an ambush which annoyed us somewhat; but when their reddish arrows began to reach the roof of my wife's wagon, I struck on them with my men so violently that they scattered at once. We killed three or four of them. The only prisoner whom we took, a youth of sixteen, when he had recovered a little from terror, pointed in turn at us and to the West, repeating the same gestures which the Yampa had made. It seemed to us that he wanted to say that there were white men near by, but it was difficult to give credit to that supposition. In time it turned out to be correct, and it is easy to imagine the astonishment and delight of my men on the following day, when, descending from an elevated plateau, we saw on a broad valley which lay at our feet, not only wagons, but houses built of freshly-cut logs. These houses formed a circle, in the centre of which rose a large shed without windows; through the middle of the plain a stream flowed; near it were herds of mules, guarded by men on horseback.

The presence of men of my own race in that valley filled me with astonishment, which soon passed into fear, when I remembered that they might be "criminal outlaws" hiding in the desert from death. I knew from experience that such outcasts push frequently to very remote and entirely desert regions, where they form detachments, on a complete military footing. Sometimes they are founders of new societies as it were, which at first live by plundering people moving to more inhabited places; but later, by a continual increase of population, they change by degrees into ordered societies. I met more than once with "outlaws" on the upper course of the Mississippi, when, as a squatter, I floated down logs to New Orleans; more than once I had bloody adventures with them, hence their cruelty and bravery were equally well known to me.

I should not have feared them had not Lillian

been with us; but at thought of the danger
in which she would be if we were defeated and
I fell, the hair rose on my head, and for the first
time in my life I was as full of fear as the greatest coward. But I was convinced that if those
men were outlaws, we could not avoid battle
in any way, and that the conflict would be more
difficult with them than with Indians.

I warned my men at once of the probable
danger, and arranged them in order of battle. I
was ready either to perish myself, or destroy
that nest of wasps, and resolved to strike the
first blow.

Meanwhile they saw us from the valley, and
two horsemen started toward us as fast as their
horses could gallop. I drew breath at that
sight, for "outlaws" would not send messengers
to meet us. In fact, it turned out that they were
riflemen of the American fur company, who had
their "summer camp" in that place. Instead
of a battle, therefore, a most hospitable recep-
tion was waiting for us, and every assistance

from those rough but honest riflemen of the desert. Indeed, they received us with open arms, and we thanked God for having looked on our misery and prepared such an agreeable resting-place.

A month and a half had passed since our departure from Big Blue River. Our strength was exhausted, our mules were only half alive; but here we might rest a whole week in perfect safety, with abundance of food for ourselves, and grass for our beasts. That was simply salvation for us.

Mr. Thorston, the chief of the camp, was a man of education and enlightenment. Knowing that I was not a common rough fellow of the prairies, he became friendly at once, and gave his own cottage to me and Lillian, whose health had suffered greatly.

I kept her two days in bed. She was so wearied that she barely opened her eyes for the first twenty-four hours; during that time I took care that nothing should disturb her. I

sat at her bedside and watched hour after hour.
In two days she was strengthened enough to
go out; but I did not let her touch any work.
My men, too, for the first few days slept like
stones, wherever each one dropped down. Only
after they had slept did we repair our wagons
and clothing and wash our linen. The honest
riflemen helped us in everything earnestly.
They were Canadians, for the greater part,
who had hired with the company. They
spent the winter in trapping beavers, killing
skunks and minks; in summer they betook
themselves to so-called "summer camps," in
which there were temporary storehouses of
furs. The skins, dressed there in some fashion,
were taken under convoy to the East. The
service of those people, who hired for a number of years, was arduous beyond calculation;
they had to go to very remote and wild places,
where all kinds of animals existed in plenty,
and where they themselves lived in continual
danger and endless warfare with redskins. It

is true that they received high wages; most
of them did not serve, however, for money,
but from love of life in the wilderness, and
adventures, of which there was never a lack.
The choice, too, was made of people of great
strength and health, capable of enduring all
toils. Their great stature, fur caps, and long
rifles reminded Lillian of Cooper's tales; hence
she looked with curiosity on the whole camp
and on all the arrangements. Their discipline
was as absolute as that of a knightly order.
Thorston, the chief agent of the company,
and at the same time their employer, main-
tained complete military authority. Withal
they were very honest people, hence time
passed for us among them with perfect comfort; our camp, too, pleased them greatly,
and they said that they had never met
such a disciplined and well-ordered caravan.
Thorston, in presence of all, praised my plan
of taking the northern route instead of that
by St. Louis and Kansas. He told us that on

that route a caravan of three hundred people, under a certain Marchwood, after numerous sufferings caused by heat and locusts, had lost all their draught-beasts, and were cut to pieces at last by the Arapahoe Indians. The Canadian riflemen had learned this from the Arapahoes themselves, whom they had beaten in a great battle, and from whom they had captured more than a hundred scalps, among others that of Marchwood himself.

This information had great influence on my people, so that old Smith, a veteran pathfinder, who from the beginning was opposed to the route through Nebraska, declared in presence of all that I was smarter than he, and that it was his part to learn of me. During our stay in the hospitable summer camp we regained our strength thoroughly. Besides Thorston, with whom I formed a lasting friendship, I made the acquaintance of Mick, famous in all the States. This man did not belong to the camp, but had wandered through the deserts with two other famous explorers, Lincoln and Kit Carson. Those three wonderful men carried on real wars with whole tribes of Indians; their skill and superhuman courage always secured them the victory. The name of Mick, of whom more than one book is written, was so terrible to the Indians, that with them his word had more weight than a United States treaty. The Government employed him often as an intermediary, and finally appointed him Governor of Oregon. When I made his acquaintance he was nearly fifty years old; but his hair was as black as the feather of a raven, and in his glance was mingled kindness of heart with strength and irrestrainable daring. He passed also for the strongest man in the United States, and when we wrestled I was the first, to the great astonishment of all, whom he failed to throw to the ground. This man with a great heart loved Lillian immensely, and blessed her, as often as he visited us. In parting he gave her a pair of beautiful little moccasins made by himself from the skin of a doe. That present was very timely, for my poor wife had not a pair of sound shoes.

At last we resumed our journey, with good omens, furnished with minute directions what canyons to take on the way, and with supplies of salt game. That was not all. The kind Thorston had taken the worst of our mules and in place of them given us his own, which were strong and well rested. Mick, who had been in California, told us real wonders not only of its wealth, but of its mild climate, its beautiful oak forests, and mountain canyons, unequalled in the United States. A great consolation entered our hearts at once, for we did not know of the trials which awaited us before entering that land of promise.

In driving away, we waved our caps long in farewell to the honest Canadians. As to me, that day of parting is graven in my

heart for the ages, since in the forenoon that
beloved star of my life, putting both arms
around my neck, began, all red with embar-
rassment and emotion, to whisper something
in my ear.   When I heard it I bent to her feet,
and, weeping with great excitement, kissed her
knees.

CHAPTER VIII.

Two weeks after leaving the summer camp, we came out on the boundary of Utah, and the journey, as of old, though not without labors, advanced more briskly than at the beginning. We had yet to pass the western part of the Rocky Mountains, forming a whole network of branches called the Wasatch Range. Two considerable streams, Green and Grand Rivers, whose union forms the immense Colorado, and numerous tributaries of those two rivers, cut the mountains in every direction,

opening in them passages which are easy
enough. By these passages we reached after
a certain time Utah Lake, where the salt lands
begin. A wonderful country surrounded us,
monotonous, gloomy ; great level valleys encircled by cliffs with blunt outlines, — these,
always alike, succeed one another, with oppressive monotony. There is in those deserts and
cliffs a certain sternness, nakedness, and torpor,
so that at sight of them the Biblical deserts
recur to one's mind. The lakes here are
brackish, their shores fruitless and barren.
There are no trees ; the ground over an
enormous expanse exudes salt and potash, or
is covered by a gray vegetation with large
felt-like leaves, which, when broken, give forth
a salt, clammy sap. That journey is weari-
some and oppressive, for whole weeks pass,
and the desert stretches on without end, and
opens into plains of eternal sameness, though
they are rocky. Our strength began to give
way again. On the prairies we were sur-

rounded by the monotony of life, here by the monotony of death.

A certain oppression and indifference to everything took gradual possession of the people. We passed Utah, — always the same lifeless lands ! We entered Nevada, — no change ! The sun burnt so fiercely that our heads were bursting from pain ; the light, reflecting from a surface covered with salt, dazzled the eye ; in the air was floating a kind of dust, coming it was unknown whence, which inflamed our eyelids. The draught-beasts, time after time, seized the earth with their teeth, and dropped from sunstroke, as if felled by lightning. The majority of the people kept themselves up only with the thought that in a week or two weeks the Sierra Nevada would appear on the horizon, and behind that the desired California.

Meanwhile days passed and weeks in ever increasing labors. In the course of a certain week we were forced to leave three wagons behind, for there were no animals to draw them.

Oh, that was a land of misfortune and misery! In Nevada the desert became deeper, and our condition still worse, for disease fell upon us.

One morning people came to inform me that Smith was sick. I went to see what his trouble was, and saw with amazement that typhus had overthrown the old miner. So many climates are not changed with impunity; severe labor, in spite of short rests, makes itself felt, and the germs of disease are developed from hardship and toil. Lillian, whom Smith loved as if she had been his own daughter, and whom he blessed on the day of our marriage, insisted on nursing him. I, weak man, trembled in my whole soul for her, but I could not forbid her to be a Christian. She sat over the sick man whole days and nights, together with Aunt Atkins and Aunt Grosvenor, who followed her example. On the second day, however, the old man lost consciousness, and on the eighth he died in Lillian's arms. I buried him, shedding ardent tears over the remains of him who had been not only my assistant and right hand in everything, but a real father to Lillian and me. We hoped that after such a sacrifice God would take pity on us; but that was merely the beginning of our trials, for that very day another miner fell ill, and almost every day after that some one lay down in a wagon, and left it only when borne on our arms to a grave.

And thus we dragged along over the desert, and after us followed the pestilence, grasping new victims continually. In her turn Aunt Atkins fell ill, but, thanks to Lillian's efforts, her sickness was conquered. The soul was dying in me every instant, and more than once, when Lillian was with the sick, and I somewhere on guard in front of the camp, alone in the darkness, I pressed my temples with my hands and knelt down in prayer to God. Obedient as a dog, I was whining for mercy on her without daring to say: "Let Thy will and not mine be done." Sometimes in the night, when we were alone, I woke suddenly, for it seemed to me that the pestilence was pushing the canvas of my wagon aside and staring in, looking for Lillian. All the intervals when I was not with her, and they formed most of the time, were for me changed into one torture, under which I bent as a tree before a whirlwind. Lillian, however, had been equal to all toils and efforts so far. Though the strongest men fell, I saw her emaciated it is true, pale, and with marks of maternity increasingly definite on her forehead, but in health, and going from wagon to wagon. I dared not even ask if she were well; I only took her by the shoulders and pressed her long and long to my breast, and even had I wished to speak, something so oppressed me, that I could not have uttered a word.

Gradually, however, hope began to enter me, and in my head were sounding no longer those terrible words of the Bible : " Who worshipped and served the creature more than the Creator."

We were nearing the western part of Nevada, where, beyond the belt of dead lakes, the salt lands and desert rocks find an end, and a belt of prairie begins, more level, greener, and very fertile. During two days' journey no one fell ill; I thought that our misery was over. And it was high time!

Nine men had died, six were ailing yet; under the fear of infection discipline had begun to relax; nearly all the horses were dead, and the mules seemed rather skeletons than beasts. Of the fifty wagons with which we had moved out of the summer camp, only thirty-two were dragging now over the desert. Besides, since no one wished to go hunting lest he might fall somewhere away from the caravan and be left without aid, our supplies, not being replenished, were coming to an end. Wishing to spare them, we had lived for a week past on black ground squirrels; but their malodorous meat had so disgusted us that we put it to our mouths with loathing, and even that wretched food was not found in sufficiency. Beyond the lakes, however, game became more frequent, and grass was abundant. Again we met Indians, who, in opposition to their custom, attacked us in daylight and on the open plain; having firearms, they killed four of our people. In the conflict I received such a severe wound in the head from a hatchet that in the evening of that day I lost consciousness from loss of blood; but I was happy since Lillian was nursing me, and not patients from whom she might catch the typhus. Three days I lay in the wagon, pleasant days, since I was with her continually. I could kiss her hands when she was changing the bandages, and look at her. On the third day I was able to sit on horseback; but the soul was weak in me, and I feigned sickness before myself so as to be with her longer.

Only then did I discover how tired I had been, and what weariness had gone out of my bones while I was lying prostrate. Before my

illness I had suffered not a little concerning
my wife. I had grown as thin as a skeleton,
and as formerly I had been looking with fear
and alarm at her, so now she was looking with
the same feelings at me. But when my head
had ceased to fall from shoulder to shoulder
there was no help for it; I had to mount the
last living horse and lead the caravan forward, especially as certain alarming signs were
surrounding us on all sides. There was a heat
wellnigh preternatural, and in the air a dull
haze as if of smoke from a distant burning; the
horizon became dull and dark. It was impossible to see the sky, and the rays of the sun
came to the earth red and sickly; the draught-
beasts showed a wonderful disquiet, and, breathing hoarsely, bared their teeth. As to us, we
inhaled fire with our breasts. The heat was
caused, as I thought, by one of those stifling
winds from the Gila desert, of which men had
told me in the East; but there was stillness
round about, and not a grass blade was stirring

on the plain. In the evening the sun went
down as red as blood, and stifling nights followed. The sick groaned for water, the dogs
howled. Whole nights I wandered around a
number of miles from the camp to make sure
that the plains were not burning; but there was
no fire in sight anywhere. I calmed myself
finally with the thought that the smoke must
be from a fire that had gone out already. In
the daytime I noticed that hares, antelopes,
buffaloes, even squirrels, were hastening east-
ward, as if fleeing from that California to which
we were going with such effort. But since the
air had become a little purer and the heat
somewhat less, I settled finally in the thought
that there had been a fire which had ceased,
that the animals were merely looking for food
in some new place. It was only needful for us
to push up as soon as possible to the burnt strip,
and learn whether the belt of fire could be
crossed or whether we should go around it.
According to my calculation it could not be

more than three hundred miles to the Sierra Nevada, or about twenty days' journey. I resolved, therefore, to reach it, even with our last effort.

We travelled at night now, for during the hours of midday heat weakened the animals greatly, and among the wagons there was always some shade in which they could rest.

One night, being unable to remain on horseback because of weariness and my wound, I sat in the wagon with Lillian. I heard all at once a sudden wheezing and biting of the wheels striking on some peculiar ground ; at the same time shouts of " Stop ! stop ! " were heard along the whole length of the train. I sprang from the wagon at once. By the light of the moon I saw the drivers bent to the earth and looking at it carefully. At the same moment a voice called :

" Ho, captain, we are travelling on coals."

I bent down, felt the earth, — we were travelling on a burnt prairie. I stopped the caravan at once, and we remained the rest of the night.

on that spot. With the first light of morning
a wonderful sight struck our eyes: As far as
we could see, there lay a plain black as coal,—
not only were all the bushes and grass burnt,
but the earth was so glossy that the feet of our
mules and the wheels of the wagons were reflected in it as they might have been in a
mirror. We could not see clearly the width of
the fire, for the horizon was still hazy from
smoke ; but I gave command without hesitation
to turn to the south, so as to reach the edge of
that tract instead of venturing on the burnt
country. I knew from experience what it is to
travel on burnt prairie land where there is not
a blade of grass for draught-beasts. Since
evidently the fire had moved northward with
the wind, I hoped by going toward the south
to reach the beginning of it.

The people obeyed my order, it is true, but
rather unwillingly, for it involved God knows
how long a delay in the journey. During our
halt at noon the smoke became thinner: but if

it did, the heat grew so terrible that the air quivered from its fervency, and all at once something took place which might seem a miracle.

On a sudden the haze and smoke parted, as if at a signal, and before our eyes rose the Sierra Nevada, green, smiling, wonderful, covered with gleaming snow on the summits, and so near that with the naked eye we could see the dents in the mountains, the green lakes, and the forests. It seemed to us that a fresh breeze filled with odors from the pitchy fir was coming to us above the burnt fields, and that in a few hours we should reach the flowery foothills. At this sight the people, worn out with the terrible desert and with labors, went out of their minds almost with delight; some fell on the ground sobbing, others stretched forth their hands toward heaven or burst into laughter, others grew pale without power to speak. Lillian and I wept from delight too, which in me was mingled with astonishment, for I had thought that a hundred and fifty miles at least separated us yet from California; but there were the mountains smiling at us across the burnt plain, and they seemed to approach as if by magic, and bend toward us and invite us and lure us on.

The hours fixed for rest had not passed yet, but the people would not hear of a longer halt. Even the sick stretched out their yellow hands from beneath the canvas roofs and begged us to harness the mules and drive on. Briskly and willingly we moved forward, and to the biting of the wheels on the charred earth were joined the cracking of whips, shouts, and songs; of driving around the burnt tract there was not a word now. Why go around when a few tens of miles farther on was California and its marvellous snowy mountains? We went straight across toward them.

Meanwhile the smoke covered the bright view from us again with a wonderful suddenness. Hours passed; the horizon came nearer. At last the sun went down ; night came. The stars twinkled dimly on the sky, but we went forward without rest ; still the mountains were evidently farther than they seemed. About midnight the mules began to squeal and balk ; an hour later the caravan stopped, for the greater number of the beasts had lain down. The men tried to raise them, but there was no chance of doing so. Not an eye closed all night. At the first rays of light our glances flew eagerly into the distance and — found nothing. A dark mourning desert extended as far as the eye could see, monotonous, dull, defining itself with a sharp line at the horizon ; of yesterday's mountains there was not a trace.

The people were amazed. To me the ominous word " mirage " explained everything, but also it went with a quiver to the marrow of my bones. What was to be done, — go on? But if that burnt plain extended for hundreds of miles? Return, and then seek some miles distant the end of the burnt tract? — but had the

mules strength to go back over the same road?
I hardly dared to look to the bottom of that
abyss, on the brink of which we were all standing. I wished, however, to know what course
to take. I mounted my horse, moved forward,
and from a neighboring elevation I took in with
my eye a wider horizon with the aid of a field-
glass. I saw in the distance a green strip. When
I reached it, however, after an hour's journey,
the place turned out to be merely a lake along
the bank of which the fire had not destroyed
vegetation completely. The burnt plain extended farther than vision through the glass.
There was no help, it was necessary to turn back
the caravan and go around the fire. For that
purpose I turned my horse. I expected to find
the wagons where I had left them, for I had
given command to wait for me there. Meanwhile, disobeying my command, they had raised
the mules, and the caravan went on. To my
questions they answered moodily : "There are
the mountains, we will go to them."

I did not try even to struggle, for I saw that there was no human power present to stop those men. Perhaps I should have gone back alone with Lillian, but my wagon was not there, and Lillian had gone on with Aunt Atkins.

We advanced. Night came again, and with it a forced halt. Out of the burnt plain rose a great lurid moon and lighted the distance, which was equally black. In the morning only half of the wagons could be moved, for the mules of the others had died. The heat of that day was dreadful. The sun's rays, absorbed by the charred land, filled the air with fire. On the road one of the sick men expired in dreadful convulsions, and no one undertook his burial; we laid him down on the plain and went farther.

The water in the lake at which I had been the day before refreshed men and animals for a time, but could not restore their strength. The mules had not nipped a grass blade for thirty-six hours, and had lived only on straw which we took out of the wagons; but even that failed them now. We marked the road as we went with their bodies, and on the third day there was left one only, which I took by force for Lillian. The wagons and the tools in them, which were to give us bread in California, remained in that desert, — be it cursed for all ages!

Every one now except Lillian went on foot. Soon a new enemy looked us in the eyes, — hunger. A part of our provisions had been left in the wagons, that which each one could carry was eaten. Meanwhile there was not a living thing in the country around us. I alone in the whole caravan had biscuits yet and a piece of salt meat; but I hid them for Lillian, and I was ready to rend any man to pieces who would mention that food. I ate nothing myself, and that terrible plain stretched on without end.

As if to add to our torments the mirage appeared in the midday hours on the plain again, showing us mountains and forests with lakes ; but the nights were more terrible than ever. All the rays which that charred land stole from the sun in the daytime came out at night, scorching our feet and parching our throats. On such a a night one man lost his mind, and sitting on the ground burst into spasmodical laughter, and that dreadful laughter followed us long in the darkness. The mule on which Lillian was riding fell ; the famishing people tore it to bits in a twinkle, but what food was that for two hundred !

The fourth day passed and the fifth. From hunger, the faces of the people became like those of birds of some kind, and they began to look with hate at one another. They knew that I had provisions ; but they knew, too, that to ask one crumb of me was death, hence the instinct of life overcame in them hunger. I gave food to Lillian only at night, so as not to enrage them with the sight of it. She implored me by all that was holy to take my share, but

I threatened to put a bullet in my brain if she even mentioned it. She was able, however, to steal from my watchfulness crumbs which she gave to Aunt Atkins and Aunt Grosvenor. At that time hunger was tearing my entrails with iron hand, and my head was burning from the wound.

For five days there had been nothing in my mouth but water from that lake. The thought that I was carrying bread and meat, that I had them with me, that I could eat, became a torture ; I was afraid besides, that being wounded, I might go mad and seize the food.

"O Lord !" cried I in spirit, "suffer me not to become so far brutalized as to touch that which is to keep her in life !" But there was no mercy above me. On the morning of the sixth day I saw on Lillian's face fiery spots ; her hands were inflamed, she panted loudly. All at once she looked at me wanderingly, and said in haste, hurrying lest she might lose presence of mind, —

"Ralph, leave me here; save yourself, there is no hope for me."

I gritted my teeth, for I wanted to howl and blaspheme; but saying nothing I took her by the hands. Fiery zigzags began to leap before my eyes in the air, and to form the words: "Who worshipped and served the creature more than the Creator?" I had broken like a bow too much bent; so, staring at the merciless heavens, I exclaimed with my whole soul in rebellion, —

"I!"

Meanwhile I was bearing to the mount of execution my dearest burden, this my only one, my saint, my beloved martyr.

I know not where I found strength; I was insensible to hunger, to heat, to suffering. I saw nothing before me, neither people nor the burning plain; I saw nothing but Lillian. That night she grew worse. She lost consciousness; at times she groaned in a low voice, —

"Ralph, water!" And oh, torments! I had

only salt meat and dry biscuits. In supreme despair I cut my arm with a knife to moisten her lips with my blood; she grew conscious, cried out, and fell into a protracted faint, from which I thought she would not recover. When she came to herself she wished to say something, but the fever had blunted her mind, and she only murmured, —

"Ralph, be not angry! I am your wife."

I carried her farther in silence. I had grown stupid from pain.

The seventh day came. The Sierra Nevada appeared at last on the horizon, and as the sun was going down the life of my life began to quench also. When she was dying I placed her on the burnt ground and knelt beside her. Her widely opened eyes were gleaming and fixed on me; thought appeared in them for a moment, and she whispered, —

"My dear, my husband!" Then a quiver ran through her, fear was on her face, — and she died.

I tore the bandages from my head, and lost consciousness. I have no memory of what happened after that. As in a kind of dream I remember people who surrounded me and took my weapons; then they dug a grave, as it were; and, still later, darkness and raving seized me, and in them the fiery words: "Who worshipped and served the creature more than the Creator!"

I woke a month later in California at the house of Moshynski, a settler. When I had come to health somewhat I set out for Nevada; the prairie had grown over again with grass, and was abundantly green, so that I could not find even her grave, and to this day I know not where her sacred remains are lying. What have I done, O God, that Thou didst turn Thy face from me and forget me in the desert? — I know not. Were it permitted me to weep even one hour at her grave, life would be easier. Every year I go to Nevada, and every year I seek in vain. Since those dreadful hours long years have passed. My wretched lips have uttered more than once, Let Thy will be done! But without her it is hard for me in the world. A man lives and walks among people, and laughs even at times; but the lonely old heart weeps and loves, and yearns and remembers.

I am old, and it is not long till I shall make another journey, the journey to eternity; and for one thing alone I ask God, — that on those celestial plains I may find my heavenly one, and not part from her ever again.

SACHEM·

IN the town of Antelope, situated on a river
of the same name in the State of Texas,
every living person was hurrying to the circus.
The inhabitants were interested all the more
since from the foundation of the town that
was the first time that a circus had come to
it with dancing women, minstrels, and rope-
walkers. The town was recent. Fifteen years
before not only was there not one house there,
but in all the region round about there were
no white people. Moreover, on the forks of
the river, on the very spot on which Antelope
was situated, stood an Indian village called

Chiavatta. That had been the capital of the Black Snakes, who in their time were such an eyesore to the neighboring settlements of Berlin, Gründenau, and Harmonia, that these settlements could endure them no longer. True, the Indians were only defending their "land," which the State government of Texas had guaranteed to them forever by the most solemn treaties; but what was that to the colonists of Berlin, Gründenau, and Harmonia? It is true that they took from the Black Snakes earth, air, and water, but they brought in civilization in return; the redskins on their part showed gratitude in their own way, — that is, by taking scalps from the heads of the Germans. Such a state of things could not be suffered. Therefore, the settlers from Berlin, Gründenau, and Harmonia assembled on a certain moonlight night to the number of four hundred, and, calling to their aid Mexicans from La Ora, fell upon sleeping Chiavatta.

The triumph of the good cause was perfect. Chiavatta was burned to ashes, and the
inhabitants, without regard to sex or age,
were cut to pieces. Only small parties of warriors escaped who at that time were absent
on a hunt. In the town itself not one soul
was left living, mainly because the place lay in
the forks of a river, which, having overflowed,
as is usual in spring-time, surrounded the settle-
ment with an impassable gulf of waters. But
the same forked position which ruined the
Indians, seemed good to the Germans. From
the forks it was difficult to escape, but the
place was defensible. Thanks to this thought,
emigration set in at once from Berlin, Gründenau, and Harmonia to the forks, in which in
the twinkle of an eye, on the site of the wild
Chiavatta, rose the civilized town of Antelope.
In five years it numbered two thousand inhabitants.

In the sixth year they discovered on the
opposite bank of the forks a quicksilver mine ;

the working of this doubled the number of inhabitants. In the seventh year, by virtue of Lynch law, they hanged on the square of the town the last twelve warriors of the Black Snakes, who were caught in the neighboring " Forest of the Dead," — and henceforth nothing remained to hinder the development of Antelope. Two " Tagblätter " (daily papers) were published in the town, and one " Montagsrevue " (Monday Review). A line of railroad united the place with Rio del Norte and San Antonio ; on Opuncia Gasse (Opuncia Street) stood three schools, one of which was a high school. On the square where they had hanged the last Black Snakes, the citizens had erected a philanthropic institution. Every Sunday the pastors taught in the churches love of one's neighbor, respect for the property of others, and similar virtues essential to a civilized society ; a certain travelling lecturer read a dissertation " On the rights of nations."

The richest inhabitants had begun to talk

of founding a university, to which the government of the State was to contribute. The
citizens were prosperous. The trade in quicksilver, oranges, barley, and wine brought them
famous profits. They were upright, thrifty,
industrious, systematic, fat. Whoever might
visit in later years Antelope with a population nearing twenty thousand would not recognize in the rich merchants of the place
those pitiless warriors who fifteen years before
had burned Chiavatta. The days passed for
them in their stores, workshops, and offices;
the evenings they spent in the beer-saloon
"Golden Sun" on Rattlesnake Street. Lis-
tening to those sounds somewhat slow and
guttural of "Mahlzeit, Mahlzeit!" (meal-
time, meal-time), to those phlegmatic "Nun ja
wissen Sie, Herr Müller, ist das aber möglich?"
(Well, now, Herr Müller, but is that possible?),
that clatter of goblets, that sound of beer
dropping on the floor, that plash of over-
flowing foam; seeing that calm, that slow-

11

ness, those Philistine faces covered with fat, those fishy eyes, — a man might suppose himself in a beer-garden in Berlin or Monachium, and not on the ruins of Chiavatta. But in the town everything was "ganz gemüthlich" (altogether cosey), and no one had a thought of the ruins. That evening the whole population was hastening to the circus, first, because after hard labor recreation is as praiseworthy as it is agreeable ; second, because the inhabitants were proud of its arrival. It is well-known that circuses do not come to every little place ; hence the arrival of the Hon. M. Dean's troupe had confirmed the greatness and magnificence of Antelope. There was, however, a third and perhaps the greatest cause of the general curiosity.

No. Two of the programme read as follows :

"A walk on a wire extended fifteen feet above the ground will be made to the accompaniment of music by the renowned gymnast Black Vulture, sachem of the Black Snakes, the last descendant of their chiefs, the last man of the tribe. 1. The walk; 2. Springs of the Antelope; 3. The death-dance and death-song."

If that "sachem" could rouse the highest interest in any place, it was surely in Antelope. Hon. M. Dean told at the "Golden Sun" how fifteen years before, on a journey to Santa Fé, he had found, on the Planos de Tornado, a dying old Indian with a boy ten years of age. The old man died from wounds and exhaustion; but before death he declared that the boy was the son of the slain sachem of the Black Snakes, and the heir to that office.

The troupe sheltered the orphan, who in time became the first acrobat in it. It was only at the "Golden Sun," however, that Hon. M. Dean learned first that Antelope was once Chiavatta, and that the famous rope-walker would exhibit himself on the grave of his fathers. This information brought the director into perfect humor; he might reckon now surely on a *great attraction*, if only he knew how to bring out the effect skilfully. Of course the Philistines of Antelope hurried to the circus to show their wives and children, imported from Germany, the last of the Black Snakes, — those wives and children who in their lives had never seen Indians, — and to say: " See, we cut to pieces men just like that fellow, fifteen years ago!" "Ach, Herr Je!" It was pleasant to hear such an exclamation of wonder from the mouth of Amalchen, or little Fritz. Throughout the town, therefore, all were repeating unceasingly, " Sachem! Sachem!"

From early morning the children were looking through cracks in the boards with curious and astonished faces; the older boys, more excited by the warrior spirit, marched home from school in terrible array, without knowing themselves why they did so.

It is eight o'clock in the evening, — a wonderful night, clear, starry. A breeze from the

suburbs brings the odor of orange groves, which
in the town is mingled with the odor of malt.
In the circus there is a blaze of light. Immense
pine-torches fixed before the principal gate are
burning and smoking. The breeze waves the
plumes of smoke and the bright flame which
illuminates the dark outlines of the building. It
is a freshly erected wooden pile, circular, with a
pointed roof, and the starry flag of America on
the summit of it. Before the gate are crowds
who could not get tickets or had not the where-
withal to buy them; they look at the wagons
of the troupe, and principally at the canvas
curtain of the great Eastern door, on which is
depicted a battle of the whites with the redskins.
At moments when the curtain is drawn aside
the bright refreshment-bar within is visible, with
its hundreds of glasses on the table. Now they
draw aside the curtain for good, and the throng
enters. The empty passages between the seats
begin to resound with the steps of people, and
soon the dark moving mass fills all the place

from the highest point to the floor.   It is clear
as day in the circus, for though they had not
been able to bring in gas pipes, a gigantic chandelier formed of fifty kerosene lamps takes its
place.   In those gleams are visible the heads
of the beer drinkers, fleshy, thrown back to give
room to their chins, the youthful faces of women,
and the pretty, wondering visages of children,
whose eyes are almost coming out of their heads
from curiosity.   But all the spectators have the
curious, self-satisfied look that is usual in an
audience at a circus.   Amid the hum of conversation interrupted by cries of " Frisch
wasser ! frisch wasser ! "   (fresh   water), all
await the beginning with impatience.

   At last a bell sounds, six grooms appear in
shining boots, and stand in two ranks at the
passage from the stables to the arena.   Between
those ranks a furious horse rushes forth, without
bridle or saddle ; and on him, as it were a
bundle of muslin ribbons and tulle, is the dancer
Lina.   They begin manœuvring to the sound

of music.   Lina is so pretty that young Matilda, daughter of the brewer on Opuncia Gasse, alarmed at sight of her beauty, inclines to the ear of Floss, a young grocer from the same street, and asks in a whisper if he loves her yet. Meanwhile the horse gallops, and puffs like an engine ; the clowns, a number of whom run after the dancer, crack whips, shout, and strike one another on the faces.   The dancer vanishes like lightning ; there is a storm of applause. What a splendid representation !   But No. One passes quickly.   No. Two is approaching.   The word "Sachem ! sachem ! " flies from mouth to mouth among the spectators.   No one gives a thought now to the clowns, who strike one another continually.   In the midst of the apish movements of the clowns, the grooms bring lofty wooden trestles several yards in height, and put them on both sides of the arena.   The band ceases to play Yankee Doodle, and gives the gloomy aria of the Commandore in Don Juan. They extend the wire from one trestle to the other. All at once a shower of red Bengal light falls at the passage, and covers the whole arena with a bloody glare. In that glare appears the terrible sachem, the last of the Black Snakes. But what is that? The sachem is not there, but the manager of the troupe himself, Hon. M. Dean. He bows to the public and raises his voice. He has the honor to beg "the kind and respected gentlemen, as well as the beautiful and no less respected ladies, to be unusually calm, give no applause, and remain perfectly still, for the chief is excited and wilder than usual." These words produce no little impression, and — a wonderful thing ! — those very citizens of Antelope who fifteen years before had destroyed Chiavatta, feel now some sort of very unpleasant sensation. A moment before, when the beautiful Lina was performing her springs on horseback, they were glad to be sitting so near, right there close to the parapet, whence they could see everything so well ; and now they look with a certain longing for the upper seats of the circus, and in spite of all laws of physics, find that the lower they are the more stifling it is.

But could that sachem remember? He was reared from years of childhood in the troupe of Hon. M. Dean, composed mainly of Germans. Had he not forgotten everything? This seemed probable. His environment and fifteen years of a circus career, the exhibition of his art, the winning of applause, must have exerted their influence.

Chiavatta, Chiavatta! But they are Germans, they are on their own soil, and think no more of the fatherland than *business* permits. Above all, man must eat and drink. This truth every Philistine must keep in mind, as well as the last of the Black Snakes.

These meditations are interrupted suddenly by a certain wild whistle in the stables, and on the arena appears the sachem expected so anxiously. A brief murmur of the crowd is heard : "That is he. that is he!" — and then silence.

But there is hissing from Bengal lights, which
burn continually at the passage. All eyes are
turned toward the chief, who in the circus will
appear on the graves of his fathers. The Indian
deserves really that men should look at him.
He seems as haughty as a king. A mantle of
white ermine — the mark of his chieftainship —
covers his figure, which is lofty, and so wild that
it brings to mind a badly tamed jaguar. He
has a face as it were forged out of bronze, like
the head of an eagle, and in his face there is a
cold gleam ; his eyes are genuinely Indian, calm,
indifferent as it were, — and ominous. He
glances around on the assembly, as if wishing
to choose a victim. Moreover, he is armed
from head to foot. On his head plumes are
waving, at his girdle he has an ax and a knife
for scalping ; but in his hand, instead of a bow,
he holds a long staff to preserve his balance
when walking on the wire. Standing in the
middle of the arena he gives forth on a sudden a war cry. *Herr Gott!* That is the cry

of the Black Snakes. Those who massacred
Chiavatta remember clearly that terrible howl,
— and what is most wonderful, those who fifteen years before had no fear of one thousand
such warriors are sweating now before one.
But behold ! the director approaches the chief
and says something to him, as if to pacify and
calm him. The wild beast feels the bit ; the
words have their influence, for after a time
the sachem is swaying on the wire. With
eyes fixed on the kerosene chandelier he advances. The wire bends much ; at moments
it is not visible, and then the Indian seems
suspended in space. He is walking as it were
upward ; he advances, retreats, and again he
advances, maintaining his balance. His extended arms covered with the mantle seem
like great wings. He totters ! he is falling ! —
No. A short interrupted bravo begins like
a storm and stops. The face of the chief becomes more and more threatening. In his
gaze fixed on the kerosene lamps is gleaming

some terrible light. There is alarm in the circus, but no one breaks the silence. Meanwhile the sachem approaches the end of the wire, stops; all at once a war-song bursts forth from his lips.

A strange thing ! The chief sings in German. But that is easy to understand. Surely he has forgotten the tongue of the Black Snakes. Moreover, no one notices that. All listen to the song, which rises and grows in volume. It is a half chant, a kind of half call, immeasurably plaintive, wild, and hoarse, full of sounds of attack.

The following words were heard : " After the great yearly rains, five hundred warriors went from Chiavatta on the war-path or to the spring hunts; when they came back from war they brought scalps, when they came back from the hunt they brought flesh and the skins of buffaloes; their wives met them with gladness, and they danced in honor of the Great Spirit.

"Chiavatta was happy. The women worked in the wigwams, the children grew up to be beautiful maidens, to be brave, fearless warriors. The warriors died on the field of glory, and went to the silver mountains to hunt with the ghosts of their fathers. Their axes were never dipped in the blood of women and children, for the warriors of Chiavatta were high-minded. Chiavatta was powerful; but pale-faces came from beyond distant waters and set fire to Chiavatta. The white warriors did not destroy the Black Snakes in battle, but they stole in as do jackals at night, they buried their knives in the bosoms of sleeping men, women, and children.

"Now there is no Chiavatta. In place of it the white men have raised their stone wigwams. The murdered nation and ruined Chiavatta cry out for vengeance."

The voice of the chief became hoarse. Standing on the wire, he seemed a red archangel of vengeance floating above the heads

of that throng of people. Evidently the director himself was afraid. A silence as of death
settled down in the circus. The chief howled
on, —

"Of the whole nation there remained only
one little child. He was weak and small, but
he swore to the spirit of the earth that he
would have vengeance, — that he would see
the corpses of white men, women, and children,
that he would see fire and blood."

The last words were changed into a bellow
of fury. In the circus murmurs were heard like
the sudden puffs of a whirlwind. Thousands of
questions without answer came to men's minds.
What will he do, that mad tiger? What is he
announcing? How will he accomplish his vengeance, — he alone? Will he stay here or
flee? Will he defend himself, and how? "Was
ist das, was ist das?" is heard in the terrified accents of women.

All at once an unearthly howl was rent from
the breast of the chief. The wire swayed vio-

lently, he sprang to the wooden trestle, standing at the chandelier, and raised his staff. A
terrible thought flew like a flash through all
heads. He will hurl around the lamps and fill
the circus with torrents of flaming kerosene.
From the breasts of the spectators one shout
was just rising; but what do they see? From
the arena the cry comes, "Stop! stop!" The
chief is gone! Has he jumped down? He has
gone through the entrance without firing the
circus! Where is he? See, he is coming,
coming a second time, panting, tired, terrible.
In his hand is a pewter plate, and extending it
to the spectators, he calls in a voice of en-
treaty: "Was gefällig für den letzten der
Schwarzen Schlangen?" (What will you give
to the last of the Black Snakes?)

A stone falls from the breasts of the spectators. You see that was all in the programme,
it was a trick of the director for effect. The
dollars and half dollars came down in a shower.
How could they say "No" to the last of the

Black Snakes, in Antelope reared on the ruins of Chiavatta? People have hearts.

After the exhibition, the sachem drank beer and ate dumplings at the " Golden Sun." His environment had exerted its influence, evidently. He found great popularity in Antelope, especially with the women, — there was even scandal about him.

YAMYOL (ANGEL)

A VILLAGE
SKETCH

YAMYOL (ANGEL)
A VILLAGE SKETCH

IN the little town of Lupiskory, after the
funeral of widow Kaliksta, there were
vespers, and after vespers old women, between
ten and twenty in number, remained in the
church to finish the hymn. It was four o'clock
in the afternoon; but, since twilight comes in
winter about that hour, it was dark in the
church. The great altar, especially, was sunk

---

[1] The Polish word for angel is *aniol*, distorted by the
old woman into *jamiol*, which is pronounced *yamyol*.

in deep shade. Only two candles were burning at the ciborium; their flickering flames barely lighted a little the gilding of the doors, and the feet of Christ, hanging on a cross higher up. Those feet were pierced with an enormous nail, and the head of that nail seemed a great point gleaming on the altar.

From other candles, just quenched, streaks of smoke were waving, filling the places behind the stalls with a purely church odor of wax.

An old man and a small boy were busied before the steps of the altar. One was sweeping; the other was stretching the carpet on the steps. At moments, when the women ceased their singing, either the angry whisper of the old man was heard scolding the boy, or the hammering on the snow-covered windows of sparrows that were cold and hungry outside.

The women were sitting on benches nearer the door. It would have been still darker had it not been for a few tallow candles, by the light of which those who had prayer-books

were reading. One of those candles lighted
well enough a banner fastened to the seat just
beyond; the banner represented sinners surrounded by devils and flames. It was impossible to see what was painted on the other
banners.

The women were not singing; they were,
rather, muttering with sleepy and tired voices
a hymn in which these words were repeated
continually, —

"And when the hour of death comes,
   Gain for us, gain from Thy Son."

That church buried in shadow, the banners
standing at the seats, the old women with their
yellow faces, the lights flickering as if oppressed by the gloom, — all that was dismal
beyond expression; nay, it was simply terrible.
The mournful words of the song about death
found there a fitting background.

After a time the singing stopped. One of
the women stood up at the seat, and began to

say, with a trembling voice, " Hail, Mary, full
of grace ! " And others responded, " The Lord
is with Thee," etc. ; but since it was the day
of Kaliksta's funeral, each " Hail, Mary," concluded with the words, " Lord, grant her eternal rest, and may endless light shine on her ! "

Marysia, the dead woman's daughter, was
sitting on a bench at the side of one of the
old women.   Just then the snow, soft and
noiseless, was falling on the fresh grave of her
mother ; but the little girl was not ten years
old yet, and seemed not to understand either
her loss, or the pity which it might rouse in
another.   Her face, with large blue eyes, had
in it the calmness of childhood, and even a
certain careless repose.   A little curiosity was
evident, — nothing beyond that.   Opening her
mouth, she looked with great attention at the
banner on which was painted hell with sinners ; then she looked into the depth of the
church, and afterward on the window at which
the sparrows were hammering.

Her eyes remained without thought. Meanwhile, the women began to mutter, sleepily, for the tenth time, —

"And when the hour of death comes."

The little girl twisted the tresses of her light-colored hair, woven into two tiny braids not thicker than mice tails. She seemed tired; but now the old man occupied her attention. He went to the middle of the church, and began to pull a knotty rope hanging from the ceiling. He was ringing for the soul of Kaliksta, but he did this in a purely mechanical manner; he was thinking, evidently, of something else.

That ringing was also a sign that vespers were ended. The women, after repeating for the last time the prayer for a happy death, went out on the square. One of them led Marysia by the hand.

"But, Kulik," asked another, "what will you do with the girl?"

"What will I do? She will go to Leschyntsi. Voytek Margula will take her. But why do you ask me?"

"What will she do in Leschyntsi?"

"My dears, the same as here. Let her go to where she came from. Even at the mansion they will take in the orphan, and let her sleep in the kitchen."

Thus conversing, they passed through the square to the inn. Darkness was increasing every moment. It was wintry, calm; the sky was covered with clouds, the air filled with moisture and wet snow. Water was dropping from the roofs; on the square lay slush formed of snow and straw. The village, with wretched and tattered houses, looked as gloomy as the church. A few windows were gleaming with light; movement had ceased, but in the inn an organ was playing.

It was playing to entice, for there was no one inside. The women entered, drank vodka; Kulik gave Marysia half a glass, saying, —

"Drink! Thou art an orphan; thou wilt not meet kindness."

The word "orphan" brought the death of Kaliksta to the minds of the women. One of them said, —

"To you, Kulik, drink! Oh, my dears, how that *paralus* [paralysis] took her so that she could n't stir! She was cold before the priest came to hear her confession."

"I told her long ago," said Kulik, "that she was spinning fine [near her end]. Last week she came to me. Said I, 'Ah, better give Marysia to the mansion!' But she said, 'I have one little daughter, and I 'll not give her to any one.' But she grew sorry, and began to sob, and then she went to the mayor to put her papers in order. She paid four zloty and six groshes. 'But I do not begrudge it for my child,' said she. My dears, but her eyes were staring, and after death they were staring still more. People wanted to close them, but could not. They say that after death, even, she was looking at her child."

" Let us drink half a quarter over this sorrow ! "

The organ was playing continually. The women began to be somewhat tender. Kulik repeated, with a voice of compassion, " Poor little thing ! poor little thing ! " and the second old woman called to mind the death of her late husband.

" When he was dying," said she, " he sighed so, oh, he sighed so, he sighed so ! — " and drawling still more, her voice passed into a chant, from a chant into the tone of the organ, till at last she bent to one side, and in following the organ began to sing, —

> " He sighed, he sighed, he sighed,
> On that day he sighed."

All at once she fell to shedding hot tears, gave the organist six groshes, and drank some more vodka. Kulik, too, was excited by tenderness, but she turned it on Marysia, —

" Remember, little orphan," said she, " what

the priest said when they were covering thy
mother with snow, that there is a yamyol [an
angel] above thee — " Here she stopped,
looked around as if astonished, and then
added, with unusual energy, " When I say that
there is a yamyol, there *is* a yamyol ! "

No one contradicted her. Marysia, blinking
with her poor, simple eyes, looked attentively
at the woman. Kulik spoke on, —

"Thou art a little orphan, that is bad for
thee ! Over orphans there is a yamyol. He
is good. Here are ten groshes for thee. Even
if thou wert to start on foot to Leschyntsi,
thou couldst go there, for he would guide
thee."

The second old woman began to sing :

"In the shade of his wings he will keep thee
    eternally,
Under his pinions thou wilt lie without danger."

"Be quiet!" said Kulik. And then she
turned again to the child, —

" Knowest thou, stupid, who is above thee ? "

" A yamyol," said, with a thin voice, the little girl.

" Oh, thou little orphan, thou precious berry, thou little worm of the Lord ! A yamyol with wings," said she, with perfect tenderness, and seizing the child she pressed her to her honest, though tipsy, bosom.

Marysia burst into weeping at once. Perhaps in her dark little head and in her heart, which knew not yet how to distinguish, there was roused some sort of perception at that moment.

The innkeeper was sleeping most soundly behind the counter ; on the candle-wicks mushrooms had grown ; the man at the organ ceased to play, for what he saw amused him.

Then there was silence, which was broken by the sudden plashing of horses' feet before the door, and a voice calling to the horses, —

" Prrr ! "

Voytek Margula walked into the inn with a

lighted lantern in his hand. He put down the lantern, began to slap his arms to warm them, and at last said to the innkeeper, —

"Give half a quarter."

"Margula, thou chestnut," cried Kulik, "thou wilt take the little girl to Leschyntsi."

"I 'll take her, for they told me to take her," replied Margula.

Then looking closely to the two women he added, —

"But ye are as drunk as — "

"May the plague choke thee," retorted Kulik. "When I tell thee to be careful with the child, be careful. She is an orphan. Knowest thou, fool, who is above her?"

Voytek did not see fit to answer that question, but determined evidently to raise another subject, and began, —

"To all of you — "

But he did n't finish, for he drank the vodka, made a wry face, and putting down the glass with dissatisfaction, said, —

"That's pure water. Give me a second from another bottle."

The innkeeper poured from another. Margula twisted his face still more :

"Ai! have n't you arrack?"

Evidently the same danger threatened Margula that threatened the women ; but at that very time, in the mansion at Lupiskory, the landowner was preparing for one of the journals a long and exhaustive article, "On the right of landowners to sell liquor, this right being considered as the basis of society." But Voytek co-operated only involuntarily to strengthen the basis of society, and that all the more because the sale here, though in a village, was really by the landowner.

When he had co-operated five times in succession he forgot, it is true, his lantern, in which the light had gone out, but he took the half-sleeping little girl by the hand, and said, —

"But come on, thou nightmare!"

The women had fallen asleep in a corner, no

one bade farewell to Marysia. The whole story was this: Her mother was in the graveyard and she was going to Leschyntsi.

Voytek and the girl went out, sat in the sleigh. Voytek cried to the horses, and they moved on. At first the sleigh dragged heavily enough through the slush of the town, but they came out very soon to fields which were broad and white. Movement was easy then; the snow barely made a noise under the sleigh-runners. The horses snorted at times, at times came the barking of dogs from a distance.

They went on and on. Voytek urged the horses, and sang through his nose, " Dog ear, remember thy promise." But soon he grew silent, and began to "carry Jews" (nod). He nodded to the right, to the left. He dreamt that they were pounding him on the shoulders in Leschyntsi, because he had lost a basket of letters; so, from time to time, he was half awake, and repeated: "To all!" Marysia did not sleep, for she was cold. She looked with widely

opened eyes on the white fields, hidden from
moment to moment by the dark shoulders of
Margula.   She thought also that her " mother
was dead ; " and thinking thus, she pictured to
herself perfectly the pale and thin face of her
mother with its staring eyes, — and she felt half
consciously that that face was greatly beloved,
that it was no longer in the world, and would
never be in Leschyntsi again.   She had seen
with her own eyes how they covered it up in
Lupiskory.   Remembering this, she would have
cried from grief; but as her knees and feet
were chilled, she began to cry from cold.

There was no frost, it is true, but the
air was penetrating, as is usual during thaws.
As to Voytek he had, at least in his stomach,
a good supply of heat taken from the inn.
The landowner at Lupiskory remarked justly :
" That vodka warms in winter, and since it is
the only consolation of our peasants, to deprive
landowners of the sole power of consoling peasants is to deprive them of influence over the

populace." Voytek was so consoled at that moment that nothing could trouble him.

Even this did not trouble him, that the horses when they came to the forest slackened their pace altogether, though the road there was better, and then walking to one side, the beasts turned over the sleigh into a ditch. He woke, it is true, but did not understand well what had happened.

Marysia begun to push him.

" Voytek ! "

" Why art thou croaking ? "

" The sleigh is turned over."

"A glass ?" asked Voytek, and went to sleep for good.

The little girl sat by the sleigh, crouching down as best she could, and remained there. But her face was soon chilled, so she began to push the sleeping man again.

" Voytek ! "

He gave no answer.

" Voytek, I want to go to the house."

13

And after a while again : " Voytek, I 'll walk there."

At last she started. It seemed to her that Leschyntsi was very near. She knew the road, too, for she had walked to church over it every Sunday with her mother. But now she had to go alone. In spite of the thaw the snow in the forest was deep, but the night was very clear. To the gleam from the snow was added light from the clouds, so that the road could be seen as in the daytime. Marysia, turning her eyes to the dark forest, could see tree-trunks very far away outlined distinctly, black, motion-less, on the white ground ; and she saw clearly also snow-drifts blown to the whole height of them. In the forest there was a certain im-mense calm, which gave solace to the child. On the branches was thick, frozen snow, and from it drops of water were trickling, striking with faint sound against the branches and twigs. But that was the only noise. All else around was still. white. silent. dumb.

The wind was not blowing. The snowy branches were not stirring with the slightest movement. Everything was sleeping in the trance of winter. It might seem that the snowy covering on the earth, and the whole silent and shrouded forest, with the pale clouds in the heavens, were all a kind of white, lifeless unity. So it is in time of thaw. Marysia was the only living thing, moving like a little black speck amid these silent greatnesses. Kind, honest forest! Those drops, which the thawing ice let down, were tears, perhaps, over the orphan. The trees are so large, but also so compassionate, above the little creature. See, she is alone, so weak and poor, in the snow, in the night, in the forest, wading along trustfully, as if there is no danger.

The clear night seems to care for her. When something so weak and helpless yields itself, trusts so perfectly in enormous power, there is a certain sweetness in the act. In that way all may be left to the will of God. The girl walked

rather long, and was wearied at last. The heavy
boots, which were too large, hindered her; her
small feet were going up and down in them
continually. It was hard to drag out such big
boots from the snow. Besides, she could not
move her hands freely, for in one of them,
closed rigidly, she held with all her strength
those ten groshes which Kulik had given her.
She feared to drop them in the snow. She began at times to cry aloud, and then she stopped
suddenly, as if wishing to know if some one
had heard her. Yes, the forest had heard her!
The thawing ice sounded monotonously and
somewhat sadly. Besides, maybe some one
else had heard her. The child went more and
more slowly. Could she go astray? How?
The road, like a white, broad, winding ribbon,
stretches into the distance, lies well marked
between two walls of dark trees. An uncon-
querable drowsiness seized the little girl.

  She stepped aside and sat down under a
tree. The lids dropped over her eyes. After a

time, she thought that her mother was coming to her along the white road from the grave-yard. No one was coming. Still, the child felt certain that some one must come. Who? A yamyol. Had n't old Kulik told her that a yamyol was above her? Marysia knew what a yamyol is. In her mother's cottage there was one painted with a shield in his hand and with wings. He would come, surely. Somehow the ice began to sound more loudly. Maybe that is the noise of his wings, scattering drops more abundantly. Stop! Some one is coming really; the snow, though soft, sounds clearly; steps are coming, and coming quietly but quickly. The child raises her sleepy eyelids with confidence.

" What is that? "

Looking at the little girl intently is a gray three-cornered face with ears, standing upright, — ugly, terrible !

THE BULL FIGHT

A REMINISCENCE OF SPAIN

THE BULL FIGHT

A Reminiscence of Spain ••

IT is Sunday! Great posters, affixed for a number of days to the corners of Puerta del Sol, Calle Alcala, and all streets on which there was considerable movement, announce to the city that to-day, " Si el tiempo lo permite " (if the weather permits), will take place bull-fight XVI., in which Cara-Ancha Lagartijo and the renowned Frascuello are to appear as "espadas" (swords).

Well, the weather permits. There was rain in the morning; but about ten o'clock the wind broke the clouds, gathered them into heaps, and drove them away off somewhere in the direction of the Escurial. Now the wind itself has ceased; the sky as far as the eye can reach is blue, and over the Puerta del Sol a bright sun is shining, — such a Madrid sun, which not only warms, not only burns, but almost bites.

Movement in the city is increasing, and on people's faces satisfaction is evident.

Two o'clock.

The square of the Puerta del Sol is emptying gradually, but crowds of people are advancing through the Calle Alcala toward the Prado. In the middle is flowing a river of carriages and vehicles. All that line of equipages is moving very slowly, for on the sidewalks there is not room enough for pedestrians, many of whom are walking along the sides of the streets and close to the carriages. The police, on white horses and in showy uniforms and three-cornered hats, preserve order.

It is Sunday, that is evident, and an afternoon hour; the toilets are carefully made, the
attire is holiday. It is evident also that the
crowds are going to some curious spectacle.
Unfortunately the throng is not at all many-
colored; no national costumes are visible, —
neither the short coats, yellow kerchiefs *à la
contrabandista,* with one end dropping down
to the shoulder, nor the round Biscay hats, nor
girdles, nor the Catalan knives behind the
girdles.

Those things may be seen yet in the neighborhood of Granada, Seville, and Cordova; but
in Madrid, especially on holidays, the cosmopol-
itan frock is predominant. Only at times do
you see a black mantilla pinned to a high comb,
and under the mantilla eyes blacker still.

In general faces are dark, glances quick,
speech loud. Gesticulation is not so passion-
ate as in Italy, where when a man laughs he
squirms like a snake, and when he is angry he
gnaws off the top of his hat; still, it is energetic

and lively.   Faces have well-defined features
and a resolute look.   It is easy to understand
that even in amusement these people retain
their special and definite character.

However, they are a people who on week-
days are full of sedateness, bordering on sloth,
sparing of words, and collected.   Sunday enliv-
ens them, as does also the hope of seeing a
bloody spectacle.

Let us cut across the Prado and enter an
alley leading to the circus.

The crowd is becoming still denser.   Here
and there shouts are rising, the people ap-
plauding single members of the company, who
are going each by himself to the circus.

Here is an omnibus filled with " capeadors,"
that is, partakers in the fight, whose whole defence is red capes with which they mislead and
irritate the bull.   Through the windows are visible black heads with pigtails, and wearing three-
cornered hats.   The coats of various colors
worn by the capeadors are embroidered with

gold and silver tinsel. These capeadors ride
in an omnibus, for the modest pay which they
get for their perilous service does not permit
a more showy conveyance.

Somewhat farther, three mounted "picadors"
push their way through the people. The sun
plays on their broad-brimmed white hats. They
are athletic in build, but bony and lean. Their
shaven faces have a stern, and, as it were, con-
centrated look. They are sitting on very high
wooden saddles, hence they are perfectly visible
over the crowd. Each of them holds in his
hand a lance, with a wooden ball at the end of
it, from which is projecting an iron point not
above half an inch long. The picador cannot
kill a bull with a weapon like that, — he can
only pierce him or stop him for a moment; but
in the last case he must have in his arm the
strength of a giant.

Looking at these men, I remember involuntarily Doré's illustrations to "Don Quixote." In
fact, each of these horsemen might serve as a

model for the knight "of the rueful visage."
That lean silhouette, outlined firmly on the sky,
high above the heads of the multitude, the
lance standing upright, and that bare-boned
horse under the rider, those purely Gothic outlines of living things, — all answer perfectly to
the conception which we form of the knight of
La Mancha, when we read the immortal work
of Cervantes.

But, the picadors pass us, and urging apart the
crowd slowly, push forward considerably. Now
only three lances are visible, three hats, and
three coats embroidered on the shoulders. New
men ride up, as incalculably similar to the first
as if some mill were making picadors for all
Spain on one pattern. There is a difference
only in the color of the horses, which, however,
are equally lean.

Our eyes turn now to the long row of carriages. Some are drawn by mules, but mules
so large, sleek, and beautiful that, in spite of the
long ears of the animals, the turn-out does not

seem ridiculous. Here and there may be seen also Andalusian horses with powerful backs, arched necks, and curved faces. Such may be seen in the pictures of battle-painters of the seventeenth century.

In the carriages are sitting the flower of Madrid society. The dresses are black, there is very black lace on the parasols, on the fans, and on the heads of ladies; black hair trimmed in forelocks, from under which are glancing eyes, as it were, of the lava of Vesuvius. Mourning colors, importance, and powder are the main traits of that society.

The faces of old and of young ladies also are covered with powder, all of them are equally frigid and pale. A great pity! Were it not for such a vile custom, their complexion would have that magnificent warm tone given by southern blood and a southern sun, and which may be admired in faces painted by Fortuni.

In the front seats of the carriages are men dressed with an elegance somewhat exaggerated ; they have a constrained and too holiday air, — in other words, they cannot wear fine garments with that free inattention which characterizes the higher society of France.

But the walls of the circus are outlined before us with growing distinctness. There is nothing especial in the building : an enormous pile reared expressly to give seats to some tens of thousands of people, — that is the whole plan of it.

Most curious is the movement near the walls. Round about, it is black from carriages, equipages, and heads of people. Towering above this dark mass, here and there, is a horseman, a policeman, or a picador in colors as brilliant as a poppy full blown.

The throng sways, opens, closes, raises its voice ; coachmen shout ; still louder shout boys selling handbills. These boys squeeze themselves in at all points among footmen and horsemen ; they are on the steps of carriages and between the wheels ; some climb up on the buttresses of the circus ; some are

on the stone columns which mark the way
for the carriages. Their curly hair, their
gleaming eyes, their expressive features, dark
faces, and torn shirts open in the bosom,
remind me of our gypsies, and of boys in
Murillo's pictures. Besides programmes some
of them sell whistles. Farther on, among the
crowds, are fruit-venders; water-sellers with
bronze kegs on their shoulders; in one place
are flower dealers; in another is heard the
sound of a guitar played by an old blind
woman led by a little girl.

Movement, uproar, laughter; fans are fluttering everywhere as if they were wings of thousands of birds; the sun pours down white light
in torrents from a spotless sky of dense blue.

Suddenly and from all sides are heard cries
of "mira, mira!" (look, look!) After a while
these cries are turned into a roar of applause,
which like real thunder flies from one extreme
to another; now it is quiet, now it rises and
extends around the whole circus.

14

What has happened? Surely the queen is approaching, and with her the court?

No! near by is heard "eviva Frascuello!" That is the most famous espada, who is coming for laurels and applause.

All eyes turn to him, and the whole throng of women push toward his carriage. The air is gleaming with flowers thrown by their hands to the feet of that favorite, that hero of every dream and imagining, that "pearl of Spain." They greet him the more warmly because he has just returned from a trip to Barcelona, where during the exhibition he astonished all barbarous Europe with thrusts of his sword; now he appears again in his beloved Madrid, more glorious, greater, — a genuine new Cid el Campeador.

Let us push through the crowd to look at the hero. First, what a carriage, what horses! More beautiful there are not in the whole of Castile. On white satin cushions sits, or re-clines, we should say, a man whose age it is difficult to determine, for his face is shaven most carefully. He is dressed in a coat of pale lily-colored satin, and knee-breeches of similar material trimmed with lace. His coat and the side seams of his breeches are glittering and sparkling from splendid embroidery, from spangles of gold and silver shining like diamonds in the sun. The most delicate laces ornament his breast. His legs, clothed in rose-colored silk stockings, he holds crossed carelessly on the front seat, — the very first athlete in the hippodrome at Paris might envy him those calves.

Madrid is vain of those calves, — and in truth she has reason.

The great man leans with one hand on the red hilt of his Catalan blade ; with the other he greets his admirers of both sexes kindly. His black hair, combed to his poll, is tied behind in a small roll, from beneath which creeps forth a short tress. That style of hair-dressing and the shaven face make him somewhat like a woman, and he reminds one besides of some actor from one of the provinces; taken generally, his face is not distinguished by intelligence, a quality which in his career would not be a hindrance, though not needed in any way.

The crowds enter the circus, and we enter with them.

Now we are in the interior. It differs from other interiors of circuses only in size and in this, — that the seats are of stone. Highest in the circle are the boxes; of these one in velvet and in gold fringe is the royal box. If no one from the court is present at the spectacle this box is occupied by the prefect of the city. Around are seated the aristocracy and high officials; opposite the royal box, on the other side of the circus, is the orchestra. Half-way up in the circus is a row of arm-chairs; stone steps form the rest of the seats. Below, around the arena, stretches a wooden paling the height of a man's shoulder. Between this paling and the first row of seats, which is raised considerably higher for the safety of the spectators, is a narrow corridor, in which the combatants take refuge, in case the bull threatens them too greatly.

One-half of the circus is buried in shadow, the other is deluged with sunlight. On every ticket, near the number of the seat, is printed " sombra " (shadow) or " sol " (sun). Evidently the tickets " sombra " cost considerably more. It is difficult to imagine how those who have " sol " tickets can endure to sit in such an atmosphere a number of hours and on those heated stone steps, with such a sun above their heads.

The places are all filled, however. Clearly the love of a bloody spectacle surpasses the fear of being roasted alive.

In northern countries the contrast between light and shadow is not so great as in Spain; in the north we find always a kind of half shade, half light, certain transition tones; here the boundary is cut off in black with a firm line without any transitions. In the illuminated half the sand seems to burn; people's faces and dresses are blazing; eyes are blinking under the excess of glare; it is simply an abyss of light, full of heat, in which everything is sparkling and gleaming excessively, every color is intensified tenfold. On the other hand, the shaded half seems cut off by some transparent curtain, woven from the darkness of night. Every man who passes from the light to the shade, makes on us the impression of a candle put out on a sudden.

At the moment when we enter, the arena is crowded with people. Before the spectacle the inhabitants of Madrid, male and female, must tread that sand on which the bloody drama is soon to be played. It seems to them that thus they take direct part, as it were, in the struggle. Numerous groups of men are standing, lighting their cigarettes and discoursing vivaciously concerning the merits of bulls from this herd or that one. Small boys tease and pursue

one another. I see how one puts under the
eyes of another a bit of red cloth, treating him
just as a "capeador" treats a bull. The boy
endures this a while patiently; at last he rolls
his eyes fiercely and runs at his opponent. The
opponent deceives him adroitly with motions of
a cape, exactly again as the capeador does the
bull. The little fellows find their spectators,
who urge them on with applause.

Along the paling pass venders of oranges
proclaiming the merits of their merchandise.
This traffic is carried on through the air. The
vender throws, at request, with unerring dexterity, an orange, even to the highest row; in
the same way he receives a copper piece, which
he catches with one hand before it touches the
earth. Loud dialogues, laughter, calls, noise,
rustling of fans, the movement of spectators as
they arrive, — all taken together form a picture
with a fulness of life of which no other spectacle can give an idea.

All at once from the orchestra come sounds

of trumpets and drums. At that signal the people on the arena fly to their places with as much haste as if danger were threatening their lives. There is a crush. But after a while all are seated. Around, it is just black: people are shoulder to shoulder, head to head. In the centre remains the arena empty, deluged with sunlight.

Opposite the royal box a gate in the paling is thrown open, and in ride two "alguazils." Their horses white, with manes and tails plaited, are as splendid as if taken from pictures. The riders themselves, wearing black velvet caps with white feathers, and doublets of similar material, with lace collars, bring to mind the incomparable canvases of Velasquez, which may be admired in the Museo del Prado. It seems to us that we are transferred to the times of knighthood long past. Both horsemen are handsome, both of showy form. They ride stirrup to stirrup, ride slowly around the whole arena to convince themselves that no incautious spectator has remained on it. At last they halt before the royal box, and with a movement full of grace uncover their heads with respect.

Whoso is in a circus for the first time will be filled with admiration at the stately, almost middle-age, ceremonial, by the apparel and dignity of the horsemen. The alguazils seem like two noble heralds, giving homage to a monarch before the beginning of a tournament. It is, in fact, a prayer for permission to open the spectacle, and at the same time a request for the key of the stables in which the bulls are confined. After a while the key is let down from the box on a gold string; the alguazils incline once again and ride away. Evidently this is a mere ceremonial, for the spectacle was authorized previously, and the bulls are confined by simple iron bolts. But the ceremony is beautiful, and they never omit it.

In a few minutes after the alguazils have vanished, the widest gate is thrown open, and a whole company enters. At the head of it

ride the same two alguazils whom we saw before
the royal box; after them advance a rank of
capeadors; after the capeadors come "banderilleros," and the procession is concluded by
picadors. This entire party is shining with all
the colors of the rainbow, gleaming from tinsel,
gold, silver, and satins of various colors. They
come out from the dark side to the sunlighted
arena, dive into the glittering light, and bloom
like flowers. The eye cannot delight itself
sufficiently with the many colors of those spots
on the golden sand.

Having reached the centre, they scatter on a
sudden, like a flock of butterflies. The picadors dispose themselves around at the paling,
and each one drawing his lance from its rest,
grasps it firmly in his right hand; the men on
foot form picturesque groups; they stand in
postures full of indifference, waiting for the
bull.

This is perhaps the most beautiful moment
of the spectacle, full of originality, so thoroughly

Spanish that regret at not being a painter comes on a man in spite of himself. How much color, what sunlight might be transferred from the palette to the canvas!

Soon blood will be flowing on that sand. In the circus it is as still as in time of sowing poppy seed, — it is barely possible to hear the sound of fans, which move only in as much as the hands holding them quiver from impatience. All eyes are turned to the door through which the bull will rush forth. Time now is counted by seconds.

Suddenly the shrill, and at the same time the mournful, sound of a trumpet is heard in the orchestra; the door of the stable opens with a crash, and the bull bursts into the arena, like a thunderbolt.

That is a lordly beast, with a powerful and splendid neck, a head comparatively short, horns enormous and turned forward. Our heavy breeder gives a poor idea of him; for though the Spanish bull is not the equal of ours

in bulk of body, he surpasses him in strength,
and, above all, in activity. At the first cast of
the eye you recognize a beast reared wild in
the midst of great spaces; consequently with all
his strength he can move almost as swiftly as a
deer. It is just this which makes him dangerous
in an unheard of degree. His forelegs are a
little higher than his hind ones; this is usual
with cattle of mountain origin. In fact, the
bulls of the circus are recruited especially from
the herds in the Sierra Morena. Their color
is for the greater part black, rarely reddish or
pied. The hair is short, and glossy as satin;
only the neck is covered somewhat with longer
and curly hair.

After he has burst into the arena, the bull
slackens his pace toward the centre, looks
with bloodshot eyes to the right, to the left, —
but this lasts barely two seconds; he sees a
group of capeadors; he lowers his head to the
ground, and hurls himself on them at random.

The capeadors scatter, like a flock of sparrows at which some man has fired small-shot. Holding behind them red capes, they circle now in the arena, with a swiftness that makes the head dizzy; they are everywhere; they glitter to the right, to the left; they are in the middle of the arena, at the paling, before the eyes of the bull, in front, behind. The red capes flutter in the air, like banners torn by the wind.

The bull scatters the capeadors in every direction; with lightning-like movements he chases one, — another thrusts a red cape under his very eyes; the bull leaves the first victim to run after a second, but before he can turn, some third one steps up. The bull rushes at that one! Distance between them decreases, the horns of the bull seem to touch the shoulder of the capeador; another twinkle of an eye and he will be nailed to the paling, — but meanwhile the man touches the top of the paling with his hand, and vanishes as if he had dropped through the earth.

What has happened? The capeador has sprung into the passage extending between the paling and the first row of seats.

The bull chooses another man; but before he has moved from his tracks the first capeador thrusts out his head from behind the paling, like a red Indian stealing to the farm of a settler, and springs to the arena again. The bull pursues more and more stubbornly those unattainable enemies, who vanish before his very horns; at last he knows where they are hidden. He collects all his strength, anger gives him speed, and he springs like a hunting-horse over the paling, certain that he will crush his foes this time like worms.

But at that very moment they hurl themselves back to the arena with the agility of chimpanzees, and the bull runs along the empty passage, seeing no one before him.

The entire first row of spectators incline through the barrier, then strike from above at the bull with canes, fans, and parasols. The public are growing excited. A bull that springs over the paling recommends himself favorably. When people in the first row applaud him with all their might, those in the upper rows clap their hands, crying, " Bravo el toro ! muy buen ! Bravo el toro ! " (Bravo the bull ! Very well, bravo the bull !)

Meanwhile he comes to an open door and runs out again to the arena. On the opposite side of it two capeadors are sitting on a step extending around the foot of the paling, and are conversing without the slightest anxiety. The bull rushes on them at once ; he is in the middle of the arena, — and they sit on without stopping their talk ; he is ten steps away, — they continue sitting as if they had not seen him ; he is five steps away, — they are still talk-ing. Cries of alarm are heard here and there in the circus ; before his very horns the two daring fellows spring, one to the right, the other to the left. The bull's horns strike the paling with a heavy blow. A storm of hand-clapping breaks out in the circus, and at that very moment these and other capeadors surround the bull again and provoke him with red capes.

His madness passes now into fury : he hurls himself forward, rushes, turns on his tracks ; every moment his horns give a thrust, every moment it seems that no human power can wrest this or that man from death.   Still the horns cut nothing but air, and the red capes are glittering on all sides ; at times one of them falls to the ground, and that second the bull in his rage drives almost all of it into the sand. But that is not enough for him, — he must search out some victim, and reach him at all costs.

Hence, with a deep bellow and with bloodshot eyes he starts to run forward at random, but halts on a sudden ; a new sight strikes his eye, — that is, a picador on horseback.

The picadors had stood hitherto on their lean horses, like statues, their lances pointing upward.   The bull, occupied solely with the hated capes, had not seen them, or if he had seen them he passed them.

Almost never does it happen that the bull begins a fight with horsemen. The capes absorb his attention and rouse all his rage. It may be, moreover, that the picadors are like his half-wild herdsmen in the Sierra Morena, whom he saw at times from a distance, and before whom he was accustomed to flee with the whole herd.

But now he has had capes enough; his fury seeks eagerly some body to pierce and on which to sate his vengeance.

For spectators not accustomed to this kind of play, a terrible moment is coming. Every one understands that blood must be shed soon.

The bull lowers his head and withdraws a number of paces, as if to gather impetus; the picador turns the horse a little, with his right side to the attacker, so the horse, having his right eye bound with a cloth, shall not push back at the moment of attack. The lance with

15

a short point is lowered in the direction of the bull; he withdraws still more. It seems to you that he will retreat altogether, and your oppressed bosom begins to breathe with more ease.

Suddenly the bull rushes forward like a rock rolling down from a mountain. In the twinkle of an eye you see the lance bent like a bow; the sharp end of it is stuck in the shoulder of the bull, — and then is enacted a thing simply dreadful: the powerful head and neck of the furious beast is lost under the belly of the horse, his horns sink their whole length in the horse's intestines; sometimes the bull lifts horse and rider, sometimes you see only the up-raised hind part of the horse, struggling convulsively in the air. Then the rider falls to the ground, the horse tumbles upon him, and you hear the creaking of the saddle; horse, rider, and saddle form one shapeless mass, which the raging bull tramples and bores with his horns.

Faces unaccustomed to the spectacle grow pale. In Barcelona and Madrid I have seen Englishwomen whose faces had become as pale as linen. Every one in the circus for the first time has the impression of a catastrophe. When the rider is seen rolled into a lump, pressed down by the weight of the saddle and the horse, and the raging beast is thrusting his horns with fury into that mass of flesh, it seems that for the man there is no salvation, and that the attendants will raise a mere bloody corpse from the sand.

But that is illusion. All that is done is in the programme of the spectacle.

Under the white leather and tinsel the rider has armor which saves him from being crushed, — he fell purposely under the horse, so that the beast should protect him with his body from the horns. In fact the bull, seeing before him the fleshy mass of the horse's belly, expends on it mainly his rage. Let me add that the duration of the catastrophe is counted by

seconds. The capeadors have attacked the
bull from every side, and he, wishing to free
himself from them, must leave his victims. He
does leave them, he chases again after the
capeadors; his steaming horns, stained with
blood, seem again to be just touching the
capeadors' shoulders. They, in escaping, lead
him to the opposite side of the arena; other
men meanwhile draw from beneath the horse
the picador, who is barely able to move under
the weight of his armor, and throw him over
the paling.

The horse too tries to raise himself: frequently he rises for a moment, but then a
ghastly sight strikes the eye. From his torn
belly hangs a whole bundle of intestines with a
rosy spleen, bluish liver, and greenish stomach.
The hapless beast tries to walk a few steps; but
his trembling feet tread on his own entrails, he
falls, digs the ground with his hoofs, shudders.
Meanwhile the attendants run up, remove the
saddle and bridle, and finish the torments of

the horse with one stab of a stiletto, at the point where head and neck come together.

On the arena remains the motionless body, which, lying now on its side, seems wonderfully flat. The intestines are carried out quickly in a basket which is somewhat like a wash-tub, and the public clap their hands with excitement. Enthusiasm begins to seize them: " Bravo el toro ! Bravo picador ! " Eyes are flashing, on faces a flush comes, a number of hats fly to the arena in honor of the picador. Meanwhile " el toro," having drawn blood once, kills a number of other horses. If his horns are buried not in the belly but under the shoulder of the horse, a stream of dark blood bursts onto the arena in an uncommon quantity; the horse rears and falls backward with his rider. A twofold danger threatens the man : the horns of the bull or, in spite of his armor, the breaking of his neck. But, as we have said. the body of the horse becomes a protection to the rider ; hence, every picador tries to receive battle at the edge of the arena, so as to be, as it were, covered between the body of the horse and the paling. When the bull withdraws, the picador advances, but only a few steps, so that the battle never takes place in the centre.

All these precautions would not avail much, and the bull would pierce the horseman at last, were it not for the capeadors. They press on the bull, draw away his attention, rush with unheard of boldness against his rage, saving each moment the life of some participant in the fight. Once I saw an espada, retreating before the raging beast, stumble against the head of a dead horse and fall on his back; death inevitable was hanging over him, the horns of the bull were just ready to pass through his breast, when suddenly between that breast and the horns the red capes were moving, and the bull flew after the capes. It may be said that were it not for that flock of chimpanzees waving red capes, the work of the picadors

would be impossible, and at every representation as many of them as of horses would
perish.

It happens rarely that a picador can stop a
bull at the point of a lance. This takes place
only when the bull advances feebly, or the
picador is gifted with gigantic strength of arms,
surpassing the measure of men. I saw two such
examples in Madrid, after which came a hurri-
cane of applause for the picador.

But usually the bull kills horses like flies;
and he is terrible when, covered with sweat,
glittering in the sun, with a neck bleeding
from lances and his horns painted red, he
runs around the arena, as if in the drunken-
ness of victory. A deep bellow comes from
his mighty lungs; at one moment he scatters
capeadors, at another he halts suddenly over
the body of a horse, now motionless, and
avenges himself on it terribly, — he raises it on
his horns, carries it around the arena, scattering drops of stiff blood on spectators in the

first row; then he casts it again on the stained
sand and pierces it a second time. It seems
to him, evidently, that the spectacle is over, and
that it has ended in his triumph.

But the spectacle has barely passed through
one-half of its course. Those picadors whose
horses have survived the defeat, ride out, it is
true, from the arena; but in place of them run
in with jumps, and amid shouts, nimble banderilleros. Every one of them in his upraised
hands has two arrows, each an ell long, ornamented, in accordance with the coat of the
man, with a blue, a green, or a red ribbon, and
ending with a barbed point, which once it is
under the skin will not come out of it. These
men begin to circle about the bull, shaking
the arrows, stretching toward him the points,
threatening and springing up toward him.
The bull rolls his bloodshot eyes, turns his
head to the right, to the left, looking to see
what new kind of enemies these are. "Ah,"
says he, evidently, to himself, "you have had

little blood, you want more — you shall have it!" and selecting the man, he rushes at him.

But what happens? The first man, instead of fleeing, runs toward the bull, — runs past his head, as if he wished to avoid him; but in that same second something seems hanging in the air like a rainbow: the man is running away empty-handed with all the strength of his legs, toward the paling, and in the neck of the bull are two colored arrows.

After a moment another pair are sticking in him, and then a third pair, — six altogether, with three colors. The neck of the beast seems now as if ornamented with a bunch of flowers, but those flowers have the most terrible thorns of any on earth. At every movement of the bull, at every turn of his head, the arrows move, shake, fly from one side of his neck to the other, and with that every point is boring into the wound. Evidently from pain the animal is falling into the madness of rage; but the more he rushes the greater his pain. Hitherto the bull was the wrong-doer, now they wrong him, and terribly. He would like to free himself from those torturing arrows; but there is no power to do that. He is growing mad from mere torment, and is harassed to the utmost. Foam covers his nostrils, his tongue is protruding; he bellows no longer, but in the short intervals between the wild shouts, the clapping, and the uproar of the spectators, you may hear his groans, which have an accent almost human. The capeadors harassed him, every picador wounded him, now the arrows are working into his wounds; thirst and heat complete his torments.

It is his luck that he did not get another kind of "banderille." If — which, however, happens rarely — the bull refuses to attack the horses and has killed none, the enraged public rise, and in the circus something in the nature of a revolution sets in. Men with their canes and women with their parasols and fans turn to the royal box; wild, hoarse voices of cruel cavaliers, and the shrill ones of senoritas, shout only one word: "Fuego! fuego! fuego!" (Fire, fire, fire!)

The representatives of the government withhold their consent for a long time. Hence "Fuego!" is heard ever more threateningly, and drowns all other voices; the threat rises to such an intensity as to make us think that the public may pass at any instant from words to a mad deed of some kind. Half an hour passes: "Fuego! fuego!" There is no help for it. The signal is given, and the unfortunate bull gets a banderille which when thrust into his neck blazes up that same instant.

The points wound in their own way, and in their own way rolls of smoke surround the head of the beast, the rattle of fireworks stuns him; great sparks fall into his wounds, small congreve rockets burst under his skin; the smell of burnt flesh and singed hair fill the arena.

In truth, cruelty can go no further; but the delight of the public rises now to its zenith. The eyes of women are covered with mist from excitement, every breast is heaving with pleasure, their heads fall backward, and between their open moist lips are gleaming white teeth. You would say that the torment of the beast is reflected in the nerves of those women with an answering degree of delight. Only in Spain can such things be seen. There is in that frenzy something hysterical, something which recalls certain Phœnician mysteries, performed on the altar of Melitta.

The daring and skill of the banderilleros surpass every measure. I saw one of them who had taken his place in the middle of the arena in an arm-chair; he had stretched his legs carelessly before him, — they were in rose-colored stockings, — he crossed them, and holding above his head a banderille, was waiting for the bull. The bull rushed at him straightway; the next instant, I saw only that the banderille was fastened in the neck, and the bull was smashing the chair with mad blows of his head. In what way the man had escaped between the chair and the horns, I know not, — that is the secret of his skill. Another banderillero, at the same representation, seizing the lance of a picador at the moment of attack, supported himself with it, and sprang over the back and whole length of the bull. The beast was dumfounded, could not understand where his victim had vanished.

A multitude of such wonders of daring and dexterity are seen at each representation.

One bull never gets more than three pairs of banderilles. When the deed is accomplished, a single trumpet is heard in the orchestra with a prolonged and sad note, — and the moment the most exciting and tragic in the spectacle approaches. All that was done hitherto was only preparation for this. Now a fourth act of the drama is played.

On the arena comes out the "matador" him-

self, — that is, the espada. He is dressed like
the other participants in the play, only more
elaborately and richly. His coat is all gold and
tinsel : costly laces adorn his breast. He may
be distinguished by this too, — that he comes
out bareheaded always. His black hair, combed
back carefully, ends on his shoulders in a small
tail.   In his left hand he holds a red cloth flag,
in his right a long Toledo sword. The capeadors surround him as soldiers their chief, ready
at all times to save him in a moment of danger,
and he approaches the bull, collected, cool, but
terrible and triumphant.

In all the spectators the hearts are throb-
bing violently, and a moment of silence sets
in.

In Barcelona and Madrid I saw the four
most eminent espadas in Spain, and in truth I
admit, that besides their cool blood, dexterity,
and training, they have a certain hypnotic
power, which acts on the animal and fills him
with mysterious alarm. The bull simply bears

himself differently before the espada from what he did before the previous participants in the play. It is not that he withdraws before him; on the contrary, he attacks him with greater insistence perhaps. But in former attacks, in addition to rage, there was evident a certain desire. He hunted, he scattered, he killed; he was as if convinced that the whole spectacle was for him, and that the question was only in this, that he should kill. Now, at sight of that cold, awful man with a sword in his hand, he convinces himself that death is there before him, that he must perish, that on that bloody sand the ghastly deed will be accomplished in some moments.

This mental state of the beast is so evident that every man can divine it. Perhaps even this, by its tragic nature, becomes the charm of the spectacle. That mighty organism, simply seething with a superabundance of vitality, of desire, of strength, is unwilling to die, will not consent to die for anything in the world! and

death, unavoidable, irresistible, is approaching;
hence unspeakable sorrow, unspeakable despair,
throbs through every movement of the bull.
He hardly notices the capeadors, whom before
he pursued with such venom; he attacks the
espada himself, but he attacks with despair
completely evident.

The espada does not kill him at once, for
that is not permitted by the rules of the play.
He deceives the bull with movements of the
flag, himself he pushes from the horns by turns
slight and insignificant; he waits for the
moment, withdraws, advances. Evidently he
wishes to sate the public; now, this very instant, he 'll strike, now he lowers his sword
again.

The struggle extends over the whole arena;
it glitters in the sun, is dark in the shade. In
the circus applause is heard, now general, now
single from the breast of some señorita who is
unable to restrain her enthusiasm. At one
moment bravos are thundering; at another, if

the espada has retreated awkwardly or given a false blow, hissing rends the ear. The bull has now given some tens of blows with his horns, — always to the flag; the public are satisfied; here and there voices are crying : " Mata el toro ! mata el toro ! " (Kill the bull ! kill the bull !)

And now a flash comes so suddenly that the eye cannot follow it ; then the group of fighters scatter, and in the neck of the bull, above the colored banderilles, is seen the red hilt of the sword. The blade has gone through the neck, and, buried two thirds of its length, is planted in the lungs of the beast.

The espada is defenceless ; the bull attacks yet, but he misleads him in the old fashion with the flag, he saves himself from the blows with half turns.

Meanwhile it seems that people have gone wild in the circus. No longer shouts, but one bellow and howl are heard, around, from above to below. All are springing from their

16

seats. To the arena are flying bouquets,
cigar-cases, hats, fans. The fight is approaching its end.

A film is coming over the eyes of the bull;
from his mouth are hanging stalactites of bloody
saliva; his groan becomes hoarse. Night is
embracing his head. The glitter and heat of
the sun concern him no longer. He attacks
yet, but as it were in a dream. It is darker
and darker for him. At last he collects the
remnant of his consciousness, backs to the
paling, totters for a moment, kneels on his
fore feet, drops on his hind ones, and begins
to die.

The espada looks at him no longer; he
has his eyes turned to the spectators, from
whom hats and cigar-cases are flying, thick
as hail; he bows; capeadors throw back to
the spectators their hats.

Meanwhile a mysterious man dressed in
black climbs over the paling in silence and
puts a stiletto in the bull, where the neck-

bone meets the skull; with a light movement he sinks it to the hilt and turns it.

That is the blow of mercy, after which the head of the bull drops on its side.

All the participants pass out. For a moment the arena is empty; on it are visible only the body of the bull and the eviscerated carcasses of four or five horses, now cold.

But after a while rush in with great speed men with mules, splendidly harnessed in yellow and red; the men attach these mules to the bodies and draw them around so that the public may enjoy the sight once again, then with speed equally great they go out through the doors of the arena.

But do not imagine that the spectacle is ended with one bull. After the first comes a second, after the second a third, and so on. In Madrid six bulls perish at a representation. In Barcelona, at the time of the fair, eight were killed.

Do not think either that the public are

wearied by the monotony of the fight. To
begin with, the fight itself is varied with personal episodes caused by temperament, the
greater or less rage of the bull, the greater or
less skill of the men in their work; secondly,
that public is never annoyed at the sight of
blood and death.

The "toreadores" (though in Spain no participant in the fight is called a toreador),
thanks to their dexterity, rarely perish; but
if that happens, the spectacle is considered
as the more splendid, and the bull receives
as much applause as the espada. Since, how
ever, accidents happen to people sometimes,
at every representation, besides the doctor,
there is present a priest with the sacrament.
That spiritual person is not among the audience, of course; but he waits in a special
room, to which the wounded are borne in
case of an accident.

Whether in time, under the influence of
civilization, bull-fights will be abandoned in

Spain, it is difficult to say. The love of those fights is very deep in the nature of the Spanish people. The higher and intelligent ranks of society take part in them gladly. The defenders of these spectacles say that in substance they are nothing more than hazardous hunting, which answers to the knightly character of the nation. But hunting is an amusement, not a career; in hunting there is no audience, — only actors; there are no throngs of women, half fainting from delight at the spectacle of torment and death; finally, in hunting no one exposes his life for hire.

Were I asked if the spectacle is beautiful, I should say yes; beautiful especially in its surroundings, — that sun, those shades, those thousands of fans at sight of which it seems as though a swarm of butterflies had settled on the seats of the circus, those eyes, those red moist lips. Beautiful is that incalculable quantity of warm and strong tones, that mass of colors, gold, tinsel, that inflamed sand, from which heat is exhaling, — finally those proofs of bold daring, and that terror hanging over the play. All that is more beautiful by far than the streams of blood and the torn bellies of the horses.

He, however, who knows these spectacles only from description, and sees them afterwards with his own eyes, cannot but think: what a wonderful people for whom the highest amusement and delight is the sight of a thing so awful, so absolute and inevitable as death. Whence comes that love? Is it simply a remnant of Middle-age cruelty; or is it that impulse which is roused in many persons, for instance at sight of a precipice, to go as near as possible to the brink, to touch that curtain, behind which begin the mystery and the pit? — that is a wonderful passion, which in certain souls becomes irresistible.

Of the Spaniards it may be said, that in

the whole course of their history they have shown a tendency to extremes. Few people have been so merciless in warfare; none have turned a religion of love into such a gloomy and bloody worship; finally, no other nation amuses itself by playing with death.

www.ingramcontent.com/pod-product-compliance
Lightning Source LLC
Chambersburg PA
CBHW011352010726
47494CB00008B/2283